KU-326-661

The Law According to Merriweather

Jacob Merriweather and his wife Marie have established thriving businesses in a growing town in California – hers as the proprietor of The Silversmith Hotel and his as the owner of a law firm. They have three children, two girls and a boy. Many years before, Jacob was a gunman, but he has put all that behind him . . . or so he thinks! Then he receives a series of threatening letters and the past comes back to haunt him, and he has to take down his Colt .44 and strap on his gunbelt . . . But is he as capable as he was?

By the same author

Shoot Out at Big King
Man of Blood
Riders from Hell
Time to Kill
Blood on the Sand
A Town Called Perdition
Incident at River Bend
The Proving of Matt Stowe
Nolan's Law
Blood Will Have Blood
Brothers in Blood
Sack Full of Dollars
Merriweather Rides West

Writing as James Dell Marr
Badland's Bounty
Horse Soldier Returns

The Law According to Merriweather

Lee Lejeune

A Black Horse Western

ROBERT HALE

© Lee Lejeune 2019
First published in Great Britain 2019

ISBN 978-0-7198-3057-0

The Crowood Press
The Stable Block
Crowood Lane
Ramsbury
Marlborough
Wiltshire SN8 2HR

www.bhwesterns.com

Robert Hale is an imprint
of The Crowood Press

The right of Lee Lejeune to be identified as
author of this work has been asserted by him
in accordance with the Copyright, Designs and
Patents Act 1988

All rights reserved. No part of this publication may be
reproduced or transmitted in any form or by any means,
electronic or mechanical, including photocopying, recording,
or any information storage and retrieval system, without
permission in writing from the publishers.

Typeset by
Derek Doyle & Associates, Shaw Heath
Printed and bound in Great Britain by
4Bind Ltd, Stevenage, SG1 2XT

CHAPTER ONE

Jacob Merriweather left his wife Marie's hotel The Silversmith early that morning for work. He owned a law firm in town, and he had a lot on his mind. Important clients to see. His assistants were loyal and capable, but he liked to keep his eye on the ball.

Jacob was tall and had always had mutton-chop whiskers, but now he ran to a beard with more than a hint of pepper and salt in it. Marie thought he looked distinguished. Few people knew about his past as a gunman further East. Jacob had put all that behind him . . . or so he thought. He still kept his Colt .44 in its holster on a hook behind the door in their private apartment in the hotel.

One day his son, Jacob Junior, asked: 'Pa, why d'you keep that gun hanging up behind the door in your room?'

'That's a long story, son, and maybe I'll tell you some day.'

'Why don't you get rid of that old thing?' Marie asked afterwards. 'You don't want your son to get ideas about killing, do you?'

Jacob grinned. 'Reminds me of the past. A man must never forget his past. That ol' shooter has kept me alive on more than one occasion. Like when I rode with Alphonso, that short-sighted amigo of mine.'

'Who happens to be lying on Boot Hill just about as dead as a man can be,' she reminded him.

'Pity he didn't see better, otherwise he'd've noticed Black Bart's resemblance to his majesty the Devil,' Jacob quipped. 'Alphonso had many faults, but he was a good buddy to me. And those were the wild days.'

'And don't forget Black Bart swung by the neck until he died after you left.'

'It didn't take long. Black Bart was so heavy his neck snapped as soon as the hangman jerked the lever. No leg pulling for him!' Jacob looked thoughtful. 'You've sure got a point there, though, Marie – but look on the sunny side. If I hadn't shot those killers in Silver Spur, they'd've shot me. And someone had to deal with that villainous rancher Jack Davidson, didn't they?'

Marie didn't contradict him, though she remembered that the rancher Davidson had been shot dead by an unknown gunman a short time after the trial in which he was found not guilty of murder.

Jacob and Marie had three children, Katie and Maisie and Jacob Junior, who was the youngest. The two girls were doing well at school, but Jacob Junior was a bit of a tear-away, full of mischief and devilment. He didn't rate school too highly – he wanted to get out into the world and make his own way. Marie had often expressed her concern.

'I don't know what's to become of that boy if he doesn't settle down.'

'Oh,' Jacob replied, 'he'll settle down soon enough.'

'Just like you, you mean,' she said with a smile.

When Jacob walked into his office, his chief clerk, Oscar, leapt up from behind his desk.

'Good morning, Boss.' He always called Jacob Boss. It was a tradition in the firm. 'There's a man waiting to see you. Says his name's Fergus Walsh. Looks pretty well heeled to me. Says he's recently moved close to town and needs a good lawyer. Shall I ask him to come through?'

'No, Oscar. In this case the mountain must go to Mohammed, especially if the guy's rich!' He gave his assistant a broad wink, which was another tradition in the firm. Though Jacob had become reasonably well-to-do, he disliked formality. And it paid off: his assistant Oscar Savage was like a second son to him.

Jacob went through to the waiting room where the prospective client was drinking coffee from a china cup.

'Ah, Mr Walsh!' Jacob said. 'So sorry to have kept you waiting. I've just arrived. What can I do for you, sir?'

Fergus Walsh set aside his cup and rose to his full height, which was about five feet six. He was somewhat younger than Jacob, but already had a considerable paunch, which was emphasized by an extremely fancy vest. 'Good morning, Mr Merriweather. They tell me you're the best lawyer in town.'

Jacob grinned. 'Something of an exaggeration, no doubt, but we do our best, Mr Walsh. I hope the coffee is to your liking?'

'Couldn't be better, Mr Merriweather. Couldn't be better.'

'So why don't you come through to my office and you can tell me what we can do for you?'

The two men walked through to Jacob's office, where they sat down on the soft seats. Indeed, the seats were so soft that a man could easily fall asleep in mid-sentence sitting in one. Almost before Fergus Walsh had his nether regions on the seat Jacob was thrusting an elaborate ebony box towards him. 'Have a cigar, Mr Walsh.'

Fergus Walsh nodded and smiled. 'I do believe I will, Mr Merriweather. I do believe I will.' As he extracted one of Jacob's best Havana cigars, Jacob noticed he had his right index finger missing, and the others were festooned with gold rings. Fergus Walsh had the aroma of wealth about him, and Jacob had a partiality for wealth, especially if it was earned by good honest labour – which, of course, it seldom was!

'Now, how can I help you, Mr Walsh?' he asked.

Fergus Walsh puffed away at his cigar and grinned, which wasn't an altogether attractive sight with his gold teeth and his fancy rings. In fact, he reminded Jacob of one of those prize pigs one sees at country fairs. 'Well, Mr Merriweather,' Walsh said, 'the fact is, I need legal advice.'

'Well, you've come to the right place, Mr Walsh. Why don't you tell me something about yourself and your needs . . . in the strictest confidence, of course.'

Fergus Walsh exhaled a large cloud of bluish cigar smoke, 'My, my, these cigars are really something else again!'

'Only the best, Mr Walsh, only the best.'

Fergus Walsh nodded. 'Why don't you have one yourself, Mr Merriweather?'

Jacob waved away the blue smoke and cleared his throat. 'To tell you the truth, Mr Walsh, I've never acquired the taste for them. Some say cigars are good for

8

the health. Others say they make you cough. I took a vow not to smoke until I was really grown up and I'm still only half way there.'

'Well,' Walsh chuckled, and then said: 'If you push up much higher, you'll reach right up to the clouds, and they say it's mighty cold up there.' He inhaled deeply and blew out another cloud of blue smoke. 'I guess you must take a drink or two from time to time, Mr Merriweather?'

'Oh, I drink, Mr Walsh. You name it and I drink it, coffee, tea, even water, though I don't care for it cold except with a tot of whisky, you know.'

Fergus Walsh gave a stuttering laugh. 'A man after my own heart, Mr Merriweather, a man after my own heart. But now to business, now to business, sir.'

'Now to business,' Jacob repeated. 'And what is your business, Mr Walsh?'

Fergus Walsh nodded and looked at his cigar as though he regretted it. 'Mr Merriweather, the fact is I have many business interests. Among other things I have interests in a silver mine. And it's quite a rich vein.'

Jacob nodded. 'That sounds like good fortune to me, sir.'

'Yes, it would be, Mr Merriweather. There's only one fly in the ointment, though, and that's my wife . . . or rather my ex-wife.'

Jacob nodded and listened. He'd learned that a man often gleans more by listening than by talking.

Fergus Walsh mumbled to himself for a moment. 'You see, Mr Merriweather, my wife Felicity and me are separated, so to speak. We can't get along together. I thought we could, but we can't.'

'Too bad,' Jacob put in. 'There's nothing like a happy

9

marriage and a good wife.'

'Too bad it is, indeed, sir. Too bad it is.' Walsh stared at Jacob for a moment with his small, pig-like eyes and looked somewhat peeved. 'Felicity is greedy, sir. She says she won't give me a divorce unless I give her half shares in my business interests!'

Merriweather nodded. 'I understand the difficulty, sir.'

'I've been foolish, Mr Merriweather,' Walsh went on, 'I've been too trusting. I thought it was a love match, but she was only after my money. A real gold digger. I see that now.'

'Indeed, sir,' Jacob said. 'So, how can I help you?'

'She's like a leech, sir, like a bloodsucking leech.'

'I understand, sir – but what about children?'

Fergus Walsh looked horrified. 'What children?'

'Have you any offspring, sir?'

'No, no, nothing like that. We haven't had any close connection of that sort for years!'

Jacob smiled. 'That's too bad, sir. So what can I do for you?'

Fergus Walsh seemed to reflect for a moment. Then he put the butt of his half-spent cigar on a convenient ashtray. 'You can help me to get rid of her, sir,' he announced with a nod of his head.

'Get rid of her,' Jacob said quietly. 'Are we talking about divorce here, Mr Walsh?'

Fergus Walsh pursed his lips and held his head on one side. 'Persuasion, Mr Merriweather. I think you understand what I'm saying to you.' His right eye drooped slightly as though he wanted to wink but couldn't quite bring himself to do it.

Jacob remained impassive: could he believe what the

man was suggesting?

Fergus Walsh looked at the stub of his cigar in the ashtray with regret. 'Of course I'd pay, Mr Merriweather. I'd pay whatever is necessary to get the job done, you understand me.'

Jacob sat back in his chair and closed his eyes for a moment, but he was far from asleep. In fact, his brain was working overtime. Then he nodded his head. 'Now, Mr Walsh, let's get things straight here. We operate a law business here. We run things strictly within the law. If you want a divorce, we might be in a position to help you. But other than that. . . .'

Fergus Walsh's piggy eyes suddenly narrowed. 'Of course, of course, Mr Merriweather. I think we have a slight misunderstanding here, sir. The law is sacred. What made you think I was suggesting anything unlawful?'

Jacob looked at him and saw something like menace in his eye. 'So you want me to write a letter telling her she'll get nothing if she persists?'

Fergus Walsh pulled a wry face. 'To start with, yes.'

'After which?' Jacob raised an enquiring eyebrow.

'Well, if she doesn't see reason we might have to employ other means.'

'What sort of means?'

Fergus Walsh shrugged. 'Like when people don't repay loans. I thought you might have someone on your staff who could just drop a hint or two, you know. . . .'

At that moment Jacob decided he didn't care too much for Fergus Walsh's style, and the sooner he got rid of him the better. So he stood up from behind his desk. 'Well now, Mr Walsh, I'm sorry to tell you we have no such someone. We don't collect rents, and we don't employ

11

what some folk call heavies. It was good of you to think of us, but I suggest you look elsewhere for help in this matter.'

Fergus Walsh rose to his feet slowly and shook his head. 'Well now, Mr Merriweather. I hope you don't come to regret this decision. I really do.' Though Walsh was grinning, Jacob had a distinct feeling the man was threatening him.

Jacob showed Fergus Walsh to the door and waited until the man had climbed into his buggy and had been driven away by the driver. Then he went back into his office where his chief clerk Oscar was standing by his desk. 'Well, Boss, how did it go?' the young man asked.

Jacob frowned. 'Well, you know, Oscar, I had a distinct impression that the man was threatening me.'

'How come?'

Jacob told him about the conversation in some detail.

Oscar smiled. 'Well, Boss, I'm not surprised. As soon as I saw the man I thought, that guy spells trouble. He might be rich, but he's as ugly as hell. Ugliness comes right out of his bones. That's what I thought.'

Jacob smiled. 'You said a mouthful there, Oscar. But why . . . ?'

'Why what, Boss?

Jacob remained silent for a moment: he was trying to weigh up the probabilities. Had this something to do with his own unfortunate past, he wondered. He pictured that Colt revolver hanging behind the door in The Silversmith Hotel, and his spine tingled as if he'd been given a mild electric shock.

*

12

Later that day Jacob had another unexpected visitor.

His receptionist Dorothy poked her head round the door. 'Excuse me, Mr Merriweather, there's a man to see you. He gave me his card.' She handed Jacob an elaborate calling card. 'Shall I tell him you're busy and send him away, or will you see him? You have about thirty minutes before Mr Collard is due.'

Jacob looked at the card and shook his head. 'Please ask him to step in, Dorothy.'

Jacob stood behind his desk and waited, and Dorothy showed the man in immediately. He was slightly above average height with gingery hair and a ginger moustache with waxed ends, like a steer's horns. He had a cheerful, fresh-faced smile. 'Good day to you, Mr Merriweather.' He stretched out his hand.

Jacob ignored the hand. 'Please sit down, Mr Avril. I see by your card that you're in the publishing business.'

'Among other things, sir,' the man acknowledged. He was around thirty years old and looked fit, as though he did fifty press-ups each morning before breakfast.

Jacob nodded. 'Please sit down, Mr Avril, and tell me what I can do for you.'

Avril gave a slight bow, drew out a chair, and sat down. 'Springfield Publishers: that's our name and that's our business, Mr Merriweather.' He gave Jacob a smile of anticipation as though he expected him to know all about the publishing business.

'So how can I help you, Mr Avril?'

The fresh-faced smile continued. 'You can help me by giving me permission to publish your memories, sir.'

'My memories, Mr Avril?' Jacob repeated.

Avril nodded. 'Your memories, Mr Merriweather. They

13

could be of considerable interest to the public, you know.'

'How come?' Jacob asked. 'I'm a lawyer, and this is my law firm. If you want me to represent you, or advise you in a matter of law, I'll be happy to do so.'

'Oh no, no, no!' Avril waved his hand as though brushing away a troublesome fly. 'That's not it at all. We're not interested in that side of your life, Mr Merriweather. We want to publish the story of your past life.'

Jacob paused and looked directly into the man's eyes – and Avril's deep blue eyes didn't waver an inch. 'Well sir,' Jacob said, 'the past is the past, and that's all behind me now.'

Avril chuckled. 'I think you're being a little over modest, Mr Merriweather. The past is never behind us. We carry it around like heavy baggage to the end of our days.'

Jacob nodded slowly. 'I see the truth in that. Tell me, how old are you, Mr Avril?'

Avril shrugged. 'I'm just thirty-five, sir.'

'Well, you talk like the Delphic Oracle or Methuselah, you know that?'

Avril held his head on one side. 'Oh, I can't foretell the future, Mr Merriweather, but I can make you an offer you can't refuse.'

Jacob nodded. 'So please tell me about this generous offer, Mr Avril.'

Avril went into business mode. 'Have you seen our publications, Mr Merriweather?'

'Well, I can read, Mr Avril, but I'm a working lawyer. So I don't have much time for reading fiction.'

'Well, we publish facts, not fiction, sir.' Avril wagged his head and smiled. 'You're a busy man, I know. So let me explain. Our publications cover a wide range of subjects, and we have just started a series on famous men of the frontier.'

'That sounds an interesting prospect,' Jacob said with a tinge of irony.

'Yes, indeed,' Avril nodded. 'And you should be among those men of the frontier, sir.'

There was a momentary pause.

'I guess you must have been researching my past, Mr Avril.'

Avril nodded. 'We have indeed, sir. We have indeed.'

'So tell me about your publications, sir.'

'You mean the Famous Men of the Frontier series?'

'That might be a good place to start.'

Avril nodded three tines as if confirming a deal. 'The best I can do is give you copies of our Men of the Frontier series.'

'Well, that would be interesting, but maybe you'd be kind enough to give me a few names.'

'Of course,' Avril said. He pushed a catalogue across the desk. 'Please read for yourself. Page ten, if my memory serves me.'

Jacob flicked through the pages until he came to page ten. He read the heading 'Men of the Great American Frontier'. Beneath it was a list of names which included Jesse James, William Boney (alias Billy the Kid) and Pat Garett. He looked up and saw that Avril was staring at him in eager expectation.

'So what do you think, sir?' Avril said.

Jacob shook his head again. 'Why have you come here, Mr Avril?' he asked.

Avril continued to smile. 'Well, like I said, sir. My business partners and I think you should be on this list. Jacob

Merriweather has a wonderful ring about it, you know, we think it would sell well, and we would offer you a generous contract and a substantial sum up front.'

Jacob nodded. 'Have a cigar, Mr Avril.' He opened his elaborate cigar box and slid it towards Avril. Avril looked a little surprised as he extracted one of Jacob's best Havana cigars. He took it to his nose and sniffed. 'My, my, this is a mighty good cigar, Mr Merriweather.'

'Take it as a symbol of my present state of life, sir.'

Avril looked perplexed. 'Can I take that as a yes, Mr Merriweather?'

Jacob shrugged. 'Take it any way you like, sir.' He reached out and rang a bell, and Dorothy appeared almost immediately.

'Yes, Mr Merriweather?'

'Please show this gentleman out, Dorothy.'

She gave a slight curtsey.

Avril looked even more perplexed. 'May I come back next week, Mr Merriweather?'

'By all means, Mr Avril. By all means.'

Avril gave a slight bow and turned.

'Enjoy the cigar, sir,' Jacob called as Avril departed.

Dorothy returned a few minutes later holding a paper. 'This message came through for you, Mr Merriweather. The boy brought it across from the telegraph office.'

'Thank you, Dorothy.' Jacob took the paper and read the message.

It said: Remember the Alamo.

'Ask Oscar to come through, will you please, Dorothy.'

'Yes, Mr Merriweather.' She bobbed and went out.

*

16

Oscar was like a son to Jacob. Jacob had hired him 'on spec' because of the sharp intelligent look in his eye and his obvious interest in everything that moved, including law breakers and the law. When he came into Jacob's office, Jacob handed him the telegraph message.

'What do you make of this, Oscar?'

Oscar read the message through and smiled. Then he said, 'The Alamo. Well, Boss, that's really interesting. I wonder who could have sent this.'

'That's the problem. We don't know who sent it, or what it means.'

'Well, Boss, I can tell you about the Alamo. Nearly one hundred and ninety Americans, including Davy Crockett and James Bowie, were killed there when the Mexican General Santa Ana and about five thousand of his soldiers surrounded the fort and stormed it. The Americans fought well, but there were no survivors.'

'You certainly know your history, Oscar. You should have been a professor in a school somewhere.'

'Except that I've wound up here, Boss.'

'So what do you think this message means?'

'Well, Boss, there's only one thing it can mean.'

'Please enlighten me, Oscar.'

Oscar picked up the paper and scrutinized it again. 'This is a threatening message, Boss. Someone in the State obviously has a big grudge against you.'

Jacob nodded. 'This message came from San Diego.'

'Well, that doesn't mean a thing, Boss. San Diego could be anywhere in the whole state of California, and that's an awful big territory. Do you know anyone with such a big grudge against you?'

Jacob's mind went back to the visitors he'd had during

17

the morning, and he felt somewhat uneasy. He thought of the short guy Fergus Walsh, who wanted his wife dead. And he thought of the publisher Avril, who wished to publish his life story in the Men of the Frontier series – but he couldn't pin down anyone in particular, though he felt a strange creepy feeling running down his spine. Then he shrugged. 'I can think of a few people, but not from these parts, Oscar.'

Oscar pulled a sceptical face. 'Doesn't have to be from round here, Boss. Could come from way back, before you took up the law and settled down.'

Jacob nodded. 'How old are you, Oscar?'

'I'm just twenty-two, Boss.'

Jacob sat back in his chair. 'Well, let me tell you something. I'm going to send you to law school so you can qualify properly in the law. Some day you're going to be a great lawyer. I can see it written in the stars.'

'Well, thank you, Boss. I don't know a thing about the stars, but that's exactly what I should like.'

Jacob smiled. 'There's one thing I've noticed about you, Oscar.'

'What's that, Boss?'

'You don't suffer unduly from modesty, do you?'

Oscar smiled. 'No, sir. A man's got to know his own worth. Otherwise he won't get anywhere in this wide world, will he?'

'I guess that's true,' Jacob conceded.

'So,' Oscar said, 'we have two problems to solve, here.'

'Please enlighten me, Oscar.'

'Well, the first problem is Dorothy.'

'How is Dorothy a problem?'

Oscar was smiling impishly. 'She won't say yes, and she

18

won't say no.'

'What do you mean?'

'Last week I asked her to marry me, and she said she'd think about it.'

Jacob held his head on one side. 'I'm not surprised, my son.'

'Why's that, Boss?'

Jacob nodded. 'Dorothy is an unusual young woman. She has the prospect of a good career in business in front of her.'

'That's true, Boss.'

'Another thing, you can't rush a woman, especially a young woman like Dorothy.'

'Well, thank you, Boss. That sounds like real good advice.'

'So what's the other problem?'

Oscar paused for a second. 'The other problem is how we find out who sent you that threatening message, and what we are going to do about it.'

'Any ideas?' Jacob asked.

'As matter of fact I have, Boss.'

'Well, give me a clue, my son. I can't wait to hear them.'

Oscar smiled. 'My brother Pete.'

Jacob turned his head and squinted at his chief clerk. 'OK, so let's get down to ground level, shall we? You came West some five years back, I understand.'

Oscar nodded. 'Sure, the whole family moved West, my ma and pa, and my brother Pete.'

'Your brother Pete! I didn't know you had a brother Pete.'

'It's a well kept secret, Boss.' He touched the side of his nose with his index finger. 'Pa is in the newspaper business,

19

or was. Used to own a newsheet back in New York State. Trouble is, he developed a taste for the rye whiskey. So he doesn't do much now. Got kind of low in spirits. So he just sits around the house hoping something will turn up. We try to keep him off the booze.'

'Well, that sounds like a real sad case. And your brother Pete?'

'Pete's completely off his nut.'

'Quite a family!'

'I tend to exaggerate, Boss – Pete's just a little cranky in the axle.'

'Tell me more.'

'Well, Pete's a couple of years younger than me. Stage struck. Wants to open his own theatre business, but he hasn't got enough green backs together yet. He needs a rich sponsor of some kind who loves the theatre.'

Jacob considered for a moment. 'So you came from New York State?'

'That is so, Boss. But we don't talk about it much.'

'Did you ever go to the theatre yourself?'

'Ha, ha! Did we ever go to the theatre? We practically lived in the theatre. My ma was a dresser. I couldn't see the point of it myself, with all the weird characters you meet there.'

'Well, now, tell me more about your brother Pete.'

'I don't like to boast, but Pete's got a brain as bright as one of those stars in the sky.'

'So how does Pete fit in here?'

Oscar nodded and smiled again. 'Pete has strange powers. He sort of goes into a trance. That's the only way I can describe it. He's so smart he outsmarts Pinkerton himself. He could have been a real good sleuth.'

'You mean he might use his immense brain power to find out who sent that threatening message?'

Oscar was still smiling impishly. 'It's worth a try, Boss.'

Jacob nodded. 'You mean, he needs a job.'

'Well, right now he's resting, like an unemployed actor. So yes, he would be glad of a job.'

Jacob paused to think. 'Ask him to come in tomorrow morning, will you?'

'I sure will, Boss. I sure will.'

CHAPTER TWO

After work Jacob walked home to their private quarters at The Silversmith Hotel where his wife and children, Katie, Maisie and Jacob Junior, were waiting for their evening meal. Jacob Junior had a hearty appetite and loved horsing around. Katie, the eldest, ate more delicately, *like a lady*, she would say, but Maisie, the younger daughter, was pickier with her food.

'You're late, Pa!' Jacob Junior said. 'Ma's waiting to dish up and we're starving!'

Jacob smiled. 'It's been a long day, young man, and I had a lot of clients to see.' He didn't mention the telegraph message he'd received, *Remember the Alamo*. 'How did school go today?' he asked.

'School's dead boring!' Jacob Junior said. 'The teacher doesn't know a thing. She can add up and take away and multiply all right, but she doesn't know a thing about the wide world. She's just an old spinster.'

'Well, you might think that,' Marie chipped in, 'but in fact, I happen to know she's no older than thirty years old, and she's walking out with Doctor Alex Deacon.'

'He should have his head examined,' Jacob Junior said.

'All they must talk about is old bones and sums. It must be like talking to the dead.'

'You're just stupid!' Katie cut in. 'Miss Bishop is a very sweet lady, and she knows a lot more than you'll ever know.'

'Not when she gives you the birch,' Jacob Junior blurted out defiantly,

'When did Miss Bishop give you the birch?' his mother asked.

Jacob Junior blushed. He'd never seen Miss Bishop give anyone the birch.

His father smiled. 'Now, Jacob, I reckon that's an untruth.'

'You mean a lie,' Katie interjected.

'We don't use that word here,' Marie said.

'Well, whatever it is, it deserves a good birching,' their father said and they all had the grace to laugh.

'We saw a strange man as we were walking back from school,' Jacob said, as if to redeem himself.

'What sort of strange man?' his father asked.

'Well, he was as tall as you and he was wearing a long black coat. He looked kinda like the Devil pretending to be a man,' Jacob Junior said. 'And I think he was wearing a gunbelt, too.'

Katie agreed. 'He was on his horse at the corner of Main Street. He looked like he was waiting for someone, and he stared straight at us and he had eyes as cold as a fish.'

'Yes,' Maisie said. 'He stared straight at us and he didn't smile. He looked kind of creepy.'

Out of the mouths of babes, Jacob thought. 'Well, make sure you stick together, and if you see him again, come to my office and tell me.'

'Yes, Pa,' Katie said.

Later, when they were alone, Jacob told Marie about the strange message he'd received about the Alamo.

Marie looked deeply puzzled. 'That was down in Texas, way back,' she said.

'It might be way back, but it's meant to be right now.'

'What do you mean?'

'It's either some kind of a joke, or a threat, and that could be serious.'

'Who could be threatening you?'

'That's what I aim to find out. Oscar thinks it might go back to the old days when I rode with the wild bunch.'

Marie nodded. 'Well, I guess that's a possibility.'

'So you'd better keep that old Derringer of yours handy in case you need it. And I'll ask Oscar to meet the kids at school and escort them home. I don't like the sound of that cold-eyed *hombre* they saw.'

Next morning Jacob took down his Colt .44 gunbelt and strapped it to his waist under his dark lawyer's coat so most people wouldn't notice it. After all, he didn't need to scare his clients unduly, did he?

When he got to the office, Oscar was already waiting for him with another young man in tow.

'This is my brother Pete,' Oscar introduced.

Pete smiled like Oscar, and he looked just as bright, if not brighter. 'Good morning, sir,' he said politely.

'Sit down, Pete.' Jacob waved in the direction of a chair opposite his desk 'I have a tight schedule, but I can give you five minutes.'

Pete sat down but he didn't look in the least nervous. In

fact he looked as bold and confident as his elder brother Oscar.

'So,' Jacob said, 'you're looking for a job in the law.'

Pete shrugged. 'Well, not exactly, sir. The fact is I just need a job to tide me over.'

'To tide you over,' Jacob repeated sceptically. 'Then it seems I've been misinformed.'

Oscar jumped in immediately. 'Not so, Boss. The fact is, Pete is bright as a regimental button and he can turn his hand to anything.'

Pete was smiling and nodding in agreement. 'My real interest is in the theatre, sir.'

'The theatre,' Jacob said. 'We have no theatre in this town, Pete.'

'No, sir, we haven't at the moment, but we will have. It's just a matter of time and funds, of course.'

'Well, I might offer you something *to tide you over,*' Jacob said with irony, 'but it'll mean running errands and taking orders from my chief clerk here.'

Pete looked at Oscar. 'Well, he's been bossing me around since I was half a knee high to a grasshopper, so it won't make a deal of difference.'

Oscar grinned. 'Pete's being a little bit over modest as usual. Like I told you, he has a brain as big as the sun, and he'd make an awful good sleuth.'

Before anything more could be said Dorothy popped her head round the door. 'This telegraph message came for you, Mr Merriweather.' She handed Jacob the message which read, *Remember Custer and the Little Big Horn.*

'Well, now this clinches it,' Jacob said to himself.

'Clinches what, Boss?' Oscar asked.

Jacob handed the message to Oscar, and Oscar read it through with care. 'D'you mind if I hand this to Pete?' he asked.

Pete read the message and his brow clouded over. 'This is no joke, Mr Merriweather. You're being threatened here.'

Oscar nodded in agreement. 'General Custer was killed near the Little Big Horn River with over one hundred of his men when Crazy Horse led a huge band of Sioux and Cheyenne warriors across the river. Custer didn't stand a chance. In my opinion he was a damned fool!'

'A fool,' Jacob said. 'That's strong language, my son.'

'Not strong enough, Boss. He should have taken care of his men, but he thought no one could put a finger on him, and that's foolishness in my book.'

Jacob nodded. 'You're right. Custer was a damned fool.'

'I don't mean you're a fool, Boss. I mean you'd be a fool if you didn't take this message seriously.'

'Well, I am taking it seriously.' Jacob drew his Colt revolver from its holster, held it up, and put it in the drawer of his desk.

The door opened and Dorothy popped her head in again. 'Sorry to interrupt but Mr Parnell is here to see you, Mr Merriweather. He's right on time.' She gave them a radiant smile.

'Show him in, Dorothy.'

Pete followed Oscar through to the outer office where Oscar reigned supreme.

'Good job the boss has such a fine sense of humour,' Oscar said.

'You mean I blew it?' Pete replied.

'No, you didn't blow it but you might have done. I think the boss liked you fine. But what do you think of the message about Custer and the Littler Big Horn River?'

'I think it's important not to give the boss a history lesson. He's in deep trouble here, and we've got to help him.'

'Any ideas?'

'As a matter of fact I do have one or two.'

Jacob never had much for lunch. He generally took a snack at his desk at around midday. That day after his snack he went through to Oscar's office and found the brothers in earnest conversation. As soon as they saw Jacob they stopped in mid-sentence.

'Hold the fort, Oscar. I'm just going across Main Street to talk to my good friend Ed Munnings,' Jacob said.

'OK, Boss.' Oscar gave him a reassuring wink.

Jacob strapped on his gunbelt and walked to the door of his office. He looked up and down Main Street and saw nothing of particular interest, so he started crossing in the direction of the sheriff's office.

Ed Munnings, the sheriff, was sitting behind his desk writing up his accounts, a job he heartily detested.

'Why, good day to you, Jake,' he piped up. He was a surprisingly short man, more than half a head shorter than Jacob, and when he strapped on his long-barrelled revolver he looked somewhat incongruous – but most people in the town respected him, except the drunks and ne'r-do-wells, of course. 'To what do I owe this pleasure?' He grinned at Jacob. 'Is this a business call or a social call?'

'Mostly business,' Jacob said, 'but I'm pleased to see you, anyway.'

'Well, sit down, my friend, and tell me what's on your mind.'

Jacob sat down and passed the two telegraph messages across the sheriff's desk. 'What do you make of these?'

Ed wasn't too strong on reading or history but he scanned through the two messages with interest. 'Where did these come from?' he asked.

'Well, the first one came from San Diego, and I'm not sure where the second one came from.'

Ed nodded. 'Someone wants to put the frighteners on you, Jake,' he concluded. 'You any idea who it could be?'

'I don't figure it would be anyone from this town, Ed. As far as I know I don't have any enemies.' He told Ed about the visitors he'd had in the last couple of days, especially Fergus Walsh who wanted to get rid of his wife, and the publisher Avril who wanted to include him in the *Men of the Frontier* series.

'Are you tempted by the offer?' Ed asked him.

Jacob grinned. 'Which one?'

Ed gave a hoot of laughter. 'There could be money in it, Jake.'

'That guy Avril said he'd offer me a whole pile of money if I agreed.'

'Well, that's something,' Ed said.

'What worries me about that is he must have been told about the past. He must know what happened way back in Platte River.'

'Maybe so,' Ed conceded. 'Either someone spilled the beans or he's been trawling through the records.'

'Either way, it makes me feel kind of creepy, you know, like there's something going on under the surface – a not too well hidden threat.'

Ed nodded slowly. 'I sure see what you mean.' He paused for a moment. 'What about the other guy, Fergus Walsh.'

Jacob paused to reflect. 'Dressed in finery like a rich dude. Said he had considerable business interests including a silver mine, and his estranged wife was greedy. So he wanted to be rid of her.'

'You mean divorce?'

Jacob frowned. 'He said by other means. That's when I showed him the door.'

'You think he was talking about someone giving her the big sleep?'

'He didn't say it in so many words, but I believe that's what he meant.'

'What do you figure this adds up to, Jake?'

'Well, look at the facts, Ed. Two mysterious telegraph messages threatening me with death, and two highly unusual visitors, one of whom wants me to get rid of his wife.'

'Well, I sure see what you're implying,' Ed said.

'You don't think I'm going off my chump, Ed?'

Ed laughed again. 'You're not crazy, Jake, if that's what you mean. You're the sanest man on earth I know. You've been a little wild in the past, I guess, but now you're right up there with the saints.'

Jacob shook his head. 'I'm not concerned so much about myself, Ed. I'm thinking of Marie and the kids.'

'Well, we must make sure they come to no harm, mustn't we?'

'That's an understatement, my friend.'

Jacob got up and the two shook hands. Ed looked somewhat dwarfish beside Jacob, but he made up for his lack of height by good sense and bullish spirits.

*

Jacob stepped out on to Main Street and looked in both directions. It was quite a hot day and there were few people on the street. He started across Main Street towards his office, but then something highly unusual occurred. A rider came out of nowhere galloping towards him hell for leather. Jacob stepped back towards the sidewalk but the man rode on towards him, and he had a gun in his hand. Jacob drew his Colt .44, but it would have been too late anyway. The man on the horse fired a single shot, and rode on in a cloud of dust.

Jacob stood with his gun in his hand.

Ed Munnings appeared at the door of the sheriff's office with his long Buntline Special Colt in his hand. 'That guy could have killed you!' he gasped.

Jacob holstered his gun. 'He could have killed me, but he didn't. In fact he didn't mean to. He just wanted to scare the crap out of me.'

Ed pointed in the direction of the retreating gunman. 'Reckon I could wing him if I took steady aim,' he said.

'Maybe you could,' Jacob admitted, though he was somewhat sceptical. A retreating figure at that range in a cloud of dust wasn't an easy target.

It was a peaceable town. So when someone fired a shot it caused quite a commotion. Everyone within earshot was on the street almost immediately.

'Who fired that shot?' someone asked.

'Don't fret yourself,' Ed reassured them. 'Just a crazy man riding through, hoping to cause a ruckus.'

'Well, he should be ashamed of himself, frightening

innocent folk like that,' a well-known woman storekeeper exclaimed.

'Bad for business, too,' a man agreed.

Oscar and Pete appeared.

'Are you OK, Boss?' Oscar asked.

'Did someone take a pop at you, Mr Merriweather?' his brother asked.

Jacob shook his head. 'Nothing to worry about, boys. Go back to the office and keep it warm.'

The two young men laughed nervously and headed back to the office.

Jacob turned to Ed. 'I figure that was the guy my kids saw staring at them yesterday. Tall and lean and wearing a dark coat. They said he looked sinister, and now we know why.'

Ed nodded slowly. 'You know what,' he said. 'I didn't catch more than a glimpse of him, but I'm sure I've seen him somewhere before.'

'Could be on a wanted poster,' Jacob said.

'I'll look through my collection,' Ed said. 'I've got a whole heap of them from all over.'

'Including me!' Jacob speculated.

Jacob walked over to The Silversmith Hotel where he met the hotel manager, Trent Oldsmere. 'Good afternoon, Mr Merriweather,' Oldsmere said. 'I heard what happened and I'm so glad you're safe. Who would do a thing like that?'

'Thank you, Trent. You'd be surprised how many crazy people there are in the world.' Jacob walked through to Marie's private apartment. She looked yellow as parchment. 'Did someone take a shot at you?' she asked in dismay.

Jacob grinned. 'It wasn't serious,' he said. 'The guy fired in the air. It wasn't close enough to take my hat off or singe my hair.'

Marie shook her head. 'This is no joke, Jacob. Someone has a big grudge against you. If they don't want to kill you, they sure want to scare the hell out of you.'

'Well, whoever they are, they're not going to succeed,' he told her.

'Mr Ted Brasino told me he saw the man, and he looked just like the man the kids saw staring at them. I' m worried, Jacob.'

Jacob nodded. 'I'll have Oscar escort the kids to and from school.'

'Does he know how to use a gun?

'He will if I teach him. Oscar's as sharp as a whole pack of needles. Ed Manning will be on the lookout, too. We mustn't let these people get to us, Marie. I think they want to discredit us and drive us out of business. And we mustn't let that happen.'

Next morning Jacob strapped on his gunbelt underneath his dark lawyer's coat and headed for his office. He kept a wary eye open, but he saw nothing unusual or suspicious. When he reached his office he unstrapped his gunbelt and slid it into the drawer of his desk.

After a minute Oscar knocked discreetly and came in. 'Good morning, Boss.'

'Good morning, Oscar. Come in, I need to talk to you.'

'Sounds serious, Boss.'

'It is serious. Sit down.'

Oscar sat down and screwed up his face in expectation. 'What's on your mind, Boss?'

'You ever handled a shooter, Oscar?'

Oscar looked doubtful. 'No, sir, I never had the need for it. Why d'you ask?'

Jacob looked him carefully in the eye. 'I need someone to escort my kids to and from school.'

Oscar nodded sagaciously. 'You mean because of that guy taking a pot shot at you yesterday?'

'If they take a shot at me, they might take a shot at the kids to spite me, and I can't take a risk on that.'

'Well, Boss, I might not be too handy with a shooter, but I can learn. It can't be too difficult – it's just a matter of loading, aiming and firing, isn't it?'

Jacob smiled. 'There's a lot more to it than that, my son. You have to learn to aim, hold your breath, and squeeze the trigger, and that's not easy when you're faced with a professional killer with eyes as cold as a fish.'

Oscar paused for a moment. 'If you teach me, Boss, I'll be happy to learn, especially to protect those sweet kids of yours.'

'Well, that's good enough for me,' Jacob said, 'but I don't want to put you at risk, my son.'

Oscar suddenly smiled again. 'What about my brother Pete?'

'What about him?'

Oscar raised his eyebrows. 'He's sitting in my office at the moment twiddling his thumbs. It would give him something useful to do.'

Jacob shook his head in surprise. 'You mean, you don't mind if he gets in the way of a bullet?'

Oscar laughed. 'Not at all, Boss. Like I told you, Pete's been in the theatre business, and that's where he learned to shoot.'

'So Pete knows how to handle a gun?'

'You bet he does. He trained as a sharpshooter. Wanted to be in William Cody's Wild West Show, but he was way too young, but he learned to shoot, anyway. I've seen him practising and he hits the can every time.'

'Well, I'll be damned!' Jacob said.

'I hope it doesn't come to that, Boss. They say the big man in the sky is very forgiving. And you've reformed, anyway.' He gave Jacob a wink. 'And now you're on the right side of the law, Boss, and that's some turnaround, if I might say so.'

Jacob chuckled without undue modesty. 'Ask Pete to come through, will you, Oscar.'

'Sure thing, Boss.'

But before Pete could come into the office, Dorothy popped her head round the door. 'Excuse me Mr Merriweather, but another telegraph message just arrived.' She handed Jacob the message.

Jacob read it through: *Remember what happened at the Ford Theatre.* Then he handed it over to Oscar. Oscar read it and shook his head.

'Well, that settles it, Boss. The Ford Theatre. That's where the actor John Wilkes Booth assassinated President Lincoln, isn't it?'

'That's one I do happen to be familiar with,' Jacob replied.

'So,' Oscar said. 'This is becoming more than a joke, isn't it? This is serious stuff, Boss. What do you think these people want of you?'

'They want my scalp, Oscar. That's what they want.'

'Well, Boss, we have to make sure they don't get it, don't we?'

Pete wasn't actually twiddling his thumbs when Oscar asked him to come through to the Boss's office. He was scribbling notes for a play he intended to write some time in the future.

'The boss wants a word with you, Pete. This could be a chance in a lifetime. So don't blow it, boy.'

Pete went through to the office. ''You sent for me, Mr Merriweather.'

'Sit down, Pete. I hear you've been twiddling your thumbs, but I have an important assignment for you.'

'Well, that's what I'm here for, Mr Merriweather. What would you like me to do?'

Jacob took his gun out of the drawer and held it up. 'Can you handle one of these?' he asked.

Pete didn't flinch. He just looked at the weapon. 'Why, that's a Colt .44 Peacemaker, so called.'

Jacob nodded. 'You didn't even blink when I took out of the drawer.'

'No, sir. I knew you wouldn't shoot me. You pointed it at the ceiling anyway. That's always a good sign.'

Jacob shoved the gun back and closed the drawer. 'Oscar tells me you're a crack shot.'

Pete shook his head. 'Something of an exaggeration, sir. I learned to shoot, sure, and I'm pretty good in the back yard shooting at old cans and things, but I never fired a shot in anger, and that's the truth.'

Jacob nodded. 'Well, let's hope you don't have to anytime soon.'

'So, what's the assignment, Mr Merriweather?'

'I want you to escort my kids from The Siversmith Hotel

to school every morning, and pick them up from school every afternoon and escort them home.'

Pete beamed. 'That will indeed be both a pleasure and a privilege, Mr Merriweather. Is there anything else?'

'You'll need a gun.'

Pete nodded. 'Not much good without one, Mr Merriweather.'

'Any preference?'

Pete looked thoughtful for a moment. 'That old Peacemaker of yours is a bit on the heavy side. A Smith and Wesson thirty-two would be more my style.'

Jacob nodded. 'Walk down to Jenner the gunsmith and choose one for yourself. But take care. We don't want you shooting yourself in the foot, do we? It could be a little embarrassing?'

'It sure could, Mr Merriweather. And thank you, sir.'

Later in the afternoon, Ed Munnings arrived in the office. Jacob was interviewing a client, so the sheriff waited in the outer office chatting to Dorothy. After five minutes Jacob opened the door. 'Please come through, Ed.'

Ed walked into Jacob's office and sat down. 'My word, Jake, you have a fine place here, don't you?'

'Well, it's pretty good,' Jacob agreed. 'This is where I see my clients. So it needs to be real smart.'

'A man could doze right off just sitting here if he didn't have important business to attend to, couldn't he?

'I guess he could,' Jacob said. 'So what is the important business, Ed?'

Maybe Ed didn't read too well, but he certainly knew about dramatic pauses. After five seconds he took a deep breath and said, 'I think I know the man who took a pop at you.'

Jacob nodded. 'Well, put me out of my misery, Ed. Who the hell is the guy?'

Ed leaned forward with his elbows on the desk. 'Well, I can't be certain, you understand. Some of those wanted posters are a little grainy and you saw the guy a lot clearer than me. So you'll have to come over to the office and see for yourself.'

Jacob nodded again. 'Yes, Ed, I'll be glad to do that. But for God's sake, take the hooks out and let me down to the ground. Who is the guy?'

There was another deep breathing exercise. 'Ever heard the name Simms?'

Jacob looked towards the window and saw Oscar's brother Pete walking across Main Street towards Jenner the gunsmiths.

He switched to Ed Munnings again. 'Mr Simms is not one of my clients.'

Ed grinned. 'I guess he wouldn't be, not if he had a price on his head.'

'So this guy Simms had a price on his head?'

Ed nodded. 'Quite a large amount.' He breathed in slowly again. 'They call him Killer Simms.'

'Killer Simms,' Jacob repeated. A distant bell began to ring in his head. 'So he's the man.'

Ed nodded. 'Simms is a hired gun. Wanted dead or alive for killing three men.'

CHAPTER THREE

The young people got along with Pete very well indeed, though Jacob Junior figured they didn't need any kind of escort.

'We're just fine as we are,' he boasted. 'Give me a gun and that guy in the black coat won't dare to come anywhere near us.'

'Don't be an ass,' his older sister Katie said. 'You couldn't scare a jack rabbit or a gopher at two yards. Pete's just a lovely man. He tells great jokes. You wouldn't see a joke if it hit you right between the eyes.'

'OK,' Jacob Junior retorted. 'Just because you're in love with Pete, it doesn't amount to a hill of beans.'

'That's stupid,' Katie said. 'It doesn't mean a thing. You couldn't hold a gun, anyway. If you tried to shoot it, you'd fall over on your back with your legs in the air.'

Jacob Junior nearly exploded with indignation. 'You silly . . .' he shouted, but he didn't use the word that came to mind.

'Well now,' Marie intervened. 'Stop squabbling. It's very kind of Oscar's brother to want to keep you from harm.'

'That's what I think,' Maisie the youngest said. 'Pete is

38

a lovely man and I love him lots.'

'You love everybody,' Jacob Junior said. 'You're just soft in the head.'

Back in the office Oscar was talking things over with Jacob Senior. 'Why don't we ask Pete about these guys who want your scalp, Boss?'

'I'm relying on hunches right now,' Jacob admitted. 'And my hunches aren't getting me far along the track.'

'Hunches can be useful,' Oscar said, 'but maybe we should give our imaginations free rein and see where they gallop off to. I'm going to ask Pete to come through. He's playing with his new toy at the moment and I don't want him to shoot himself. It could be dangerous.'

Pete was, in fact, oiling his new Smith & Wesson, of which he was inordinately proud.

He laid the weapon on a clean cloth and came through immediately.

'What can I do for you, Mr Merriweather?'

'Please sit down and listen,' Oscar said. 'The boss needs your assistance.'

'Always glad to be of service,' Pete said, saluting with one finger above his right eye.

'Put your imagination hat on and open up your brain,' Oscar instructed.

'What would you like me to think about?'

'Just empty your brain box and hope for something to float in like when you have one of your spells, brother.'

'I don't have spells!' Pete said indignantly, 'I have brain-storms – but I'll do my best.' He sat down and closed his eyes.

Oscar turned to Jacob. 'Now, Boss, we have to keep very

quiet and still, and wait and see what he comes up with.'

Jacob said nothing. He wasn't greatly impressed by the world of spirits and things that go bump in the night, but he prided himself on his open mindedness – and after all, Pete had proved himself to be somewhat unusual, hadn't he?

They sat for several minutes in quiet expectation. Pete had his eyes closed and he swayed a little in his chair. Then his eyelids fluttered and he suddenly sparked up. 'Tell you something. What if this whole thing is nothing but a yarn, like in a stage production?' he asked.

'Is that all you can come up with, Pete?' Oscar asked him

'I'm speculating,' Pete replied. 'Like you said, I'm waiting for something to float into my head.'

'Well, as soon as something does, give us the low-down,' Oscar said.

Pete closed his eyes again for a second or two and then opened them. 'I'm playing a guessing game, here,' he said.

'Well, spit it out, boy, spit out your guesses,' Oscar demanded.

'Give me another minute,' Pete said. 'I see better with my eyes closed.'

'He sees pictures going past like a magic lantern show,' Oscar told Jacob. 'Sounds sort of crazy, doesn't it?'

Jacob looked at the clock and saw he had five minutes before his next client. He thought this ridiculous charade had gone on for far too long.

Pete swayed a little in his chair and seemed to fall into a trancelike state. 'I see a big ranch,' he muttered. 'And I see a big ranch house. Inside there are a lot of fancy chandeliers and stuff.'

'Well, that sounds like a fairy tale to me,' Oscar mocked. 'Get real, brother. Do you see a handsome prince and a fairy queen?'

Pete gave a start. 'Now I see a fat man in a fancy vest.'

'Well, that doesn't sound like Prince Charming, does it?' Oscar laughed. 'So get real, brother, and stop playing games.'

Jacob held up his hand. 'Hold on! Is that all you see, Pete?'

Pete paused for a moment and then shivered as though a chill wind had blown through the room. 'Now I see something else. The fat man is on the stairs but he's fallen on his face and there's blood on the floor. I think he's been shot.' Pete suddenly opened his eyes and shuddered. 'That was a truly terrible sight, Mr Merriweather. I think the fat guy had been murdered.'

Jacob stared at Pete. 'Well, now, that's a really interesting picture you paint.'

'Like I said, it's like a magic lantern show, except for the blood.' Oscar said.

Jacob's eyes were narrow with interest. 'That was no magic lantern show. That was real life.' He looked at Pete in wonderment. 'Do you read the news-sheets, Pete?'

'From time to time, Mr Merriweather, but only the local paper and theatre pages.'

'Does this ring a bell in your mind, Boss?' Oscar asked.

Jacob shook his head. 'That guy lying dead on the stairs sounded like the rancher Jack Davidson.'

There was a moment of stunned silence.

'Well, I'll be damned!' Oscar said.

'Yes,' Pete agreed, 'but not just yet. You have a ways to go.' He opened his eyes. 'I'm afraid that's the best I can do, Mr Merriweather.'

'Well, that's pretty good and very helpful,' Jacob said. 'Are you sure you didn't read about the Davidson case in the news-sheets?'

Pete shook his head. 'I don't think so, Mr Merriweather. Maybe I did read it somewhere and it stuck in the back of my mind.'

'Well, however it happened, it's sure given me something to chew on,' Jacob said.

'Me too,' Oscar agreed. 'I remember reading about the case. That fat guy, the rancher Jack Davidson, was shot dead with his manservant, and they never found out who fired the shots, did they?'

'No, they didn't,' Jacob affirmed.

'And if I remember right, a man by the name of Merriweather stood for the prosecution some time before.' He gave Jacob a quizzical look.

Jacob grinned. 'Your memory serves you well, Oscar. I acted as prosecutor at Jack Davidson's trial for the murder of your people on their smallholding, but then it went on to the higher court, and Davidson had the greenbacks to hire the best lawyers in the state and he got off scot free.'

'Didn't do him a whole lot of good though, did it?' Oscar said. 'Not long after that, the masked gunman broke into the ranch house and shot him dead. And nobody ever found out who'd killed him.'

Jacob nodded.

'So what are you thinking, Boss?'

'I'm thinking Mr Clavell will be here to see me, if he's on time. So we'll talk about it later.'

Right on cue, Dorothy popped her head in. 'Mr

Clavell's here to see you, Boss.'

'Ask him to step in, Dorothy. I'll see him right away.'

Cy Clavell, a man of modest proportions and smug countenance, had a benign manner which served him well both socially and in business. He was in the process of closing a deal for a substantial property on Main Street where he intended to set up a store which sold everything from bootlaces to pots and pans and ladies' and gent's clothing. He was, you might say, a man on the way up.

'*Bonjour, Monsieur,*' he said, somewhat pretentiously. 'How are things progressing, sir?'

'Things are progressing pretty well, Mr Clavell. We've had some difficulty in contacting the present owner of the property, but now that's settled and I will have my chief clerk draw up the contract immediately.'

'Good, good,' Clavell said. 'My business will put this town right on the map, you know.'

Jacob didn't disagree. He knew Cy Clavell was a man of huge ambitions. He had his sights on the governorship, and maybe something even higher.

'By the way,' Clavell said after a moment, 'I heard a man tried to shoot you the other day, and right in the middle of town, too.'

Jacob looked faintly amused. 'Well, people in my profession tend to make enemies, sir, but it was more to put the frighteners on me than to shoot me.'

'Well, I'm real glad to hear that, sir, real glad, and I'm sure glad he didn't succeed in that. But I imagine you don't scare easily, sir.' He got up from his chair and offered Jacob his hand. 'By the way, I'm staying the night at The Silversmith Hotel. Perhaps you'd be kind enough

43

to join me for dinner tonight?'

Jacob took his hand and gave it a brief but firm shake. 'Be glad to, Mr Clavell. It will be a pleasure, sir.'

Later Jacob sat behind his desk eating his frugal lunch. Dorothy popped her head round the door. 'Sorry to disturb you at lunch, Boss, but there's a man to see you. His name's Avril. He came a few days back and he's very insistent. Shall I send him away?'

Jacob thought for a moment and then nodded. 'No, Dorothy. Send him right in. I'll see him now.'

Dorothy looked slightly perplexed; it didn't seem right that Jacob should see a man while he was having his lunch. She thought it was somewhat undignified.

A moment later she showed the fresh-faced publisher in.

Jacob raised his hand. 'Please sit down, Mr Avril. I was just finishing my lunch.'

'I do apologise, sir. Maybe I should come back later?'

'No, sir. I'm happy to see you now. I've finished lunch, anyway.'

Avril sat down and gave Jacob that innocent cherubic look Jacob had seen before. 'So have you considered my offer, Mr Merriweather?'

'I'm still chewing it over, Mr Avril, but first I need to ask you a question, sir.'

'Indeed.' Avril looked delighted. 'So what's the question, Mr Merriweather?'

Jacob gave him a direct look, the sort of look that lawbreakers find quite intimidating. 'Who told you about my past activities, Mr Avril?'

Avril continued to smile. 'We do our research, Mr

Merriweather. I went back through the old news-sheets and read up on your exploits.'

'Is that all?' Jacob asked pointedly.

Avril hesitated for a moment. 'Well, there was something else, Mr Merriweather.'

'I guessed there would be. So please enlighten me on that something else.'

A look of slight embarrassment clouded Avril's face briefly but then the sun came out again almost immediately. 'I received a message, Mr Merriweather. It came by post.'

'Do you have it with you, Mr Avril?'

Avril shook his head. 'No, sir, but I remember the gist of it.'

Jacob nodded. 'Please be kind enough to tell me what it said.'

'It said, "Remember the gunman Jacob Merriweather who rode with Black Bart." Sorry to put it so bluntly, Mr Merriweather, but that's what it said.'

Jacob sat back in his chair. 'Maybe you'll be kind enough to bring the letter with you next time you come.'

'Of course,' Avril said. 'So that means you'll see me again, does it?'

'I hope so,' Jacob said. 'I really hope so.' He reached forwards and rang a bell on his desk, and Dorothy appeared immediately.

'Please show Mr Avril out, Dorothy.'

Avril was still smiling but it was a smile of bafflement.

It was the end of Jacob's working day and he was getting ready to go home when Oscar knocked and came into his office.

'I've prepared the contract for Mr Clavell, Boss. Dorothy's typing it up right now.'

'That's excellent, Oscar. Mr Clavell has big plans for this town.'

'That's good news, Boss. It means more business for us all. By the way, the answer's yes.'

'Who said yes?'

Oscar grinned. 'Dorothy consented to be my wife.'

'Well, I'm very happy for you, Oscar. What turned her round?'

'I told her I was going to law school, and that clinched the deal. She thinks I'll be a great lawyer some day.'

'And I hope she's right, my son.'

'My brother Pete has gone off to escort your kids home from school. He's really taken a shine to them, and they seem to like him, too, though Jacob Junior is a little sassy.'

Jacob grinned. 'Jacob Junior thinks he's the top hand around here, but he'll get used to the situation.

'Yes, Boss, I guess you're right.'

Jacob opened the door of his office and looked up and down Main Street. One or two men and women were passing in their buggies. He saw his three children walking with Pete further down Main Street, but otherwise all seemed quiet. So he strode across the street to Sheriff Munnings' office. Ed Munnings was sitting behind the desk that was his pride and joy. Behind him, pinned to a display board, was what he called his 'Rogues Gallery', which consisted of a number of men's faces, most of them grainy and somewhat unflattering.

'Guess which one is Killer Simms,' the sheriff said to Jacob.

Jacob didn't need a second glance. He pointed straight at the face of the man who had ridden down Main Street and fired a shot over his head. 'That's the man,' he said, jabbing a finger at the gunman's face.

'Yes, that's him,' Ed Munnings agreed. 'He's one of the old breed, a gun for hire. You pay him well, he does his job. The question is, who hired him to take a pop at you, and why didn't he shoot to kill?'

'That's a very interesting question,' Jacob said. 'I think he didn't shoot to kill because they want me alive for some reason or other.'

'But who could want that?' the sheriff asked.

'A few people I could name,' Jacob speculated, 'but they're mostly from the past.' He told Ed about Pete and the trance-like state he'd fallen into. 'I don't go much on the world of spirits and ghouls,' he said, 'but Pete gave an excellent description of the rancher Jack Davidson as he lay dead in his own blood.'

'Well, bless my cotton socks!' Ed said, 'That boy is really weird.'

'He is weird, but he's as bright as a candle on a winter night,' Jacob affirmed, 'but that description was just as it happened. He could have been talking straight out of a photograph.'

'You think he might have been looking through old news-sheets and came across a news report?'

Jacob grinned. 'He said he didn't read the news-sheets – but it makes no difference. He described the scene exactly as it happened.'

Ed drummed on his desk with his fingers. 'So, what's your theory, Jake?'

Jacob nodded. 'My theory is that someone is paying

that guy Simms to put the frighteners on me, and that someone might be connected to Jack Davidson.'

'So . . .' Ed sat back in his chair. 'We have two questions here. The first is, who is hiring Killer Simms? The second is, what do they aim to do next?'

Jacob nodded. 'And there's another question in my mind: how do we stop these people before they stop us?'

Ed stopped drumming on his desk and looked up. 'If that guy Simms is operating in my territory it's up to me as sheriff to bring him to justice. You don't get "Killer" attached to your name for nothing, do you? That guy is wanted for murder and he's operating right under my nose. So I have to do something about it, don't I?'

'That's true, Ed. And there's another thing to consider.'

'You mean he must have somewhere close where he can put his head down and rest up nights.'

Jacob nodded. 'And that can't be too far off. We track him down and we might find a nest of vipers with someone close to Jack Davidson sitting there right in the middle.'

Ed ran his fingers over his stubbly chin. 'Well, one thing's for sure, Jake: whoever's bugging you must have enough money to bury himself up to his ears in dollars.'

'Like he might own a silver mine,' Jacob speculated.

'That's true, Jake, that's true. And he must be quite an educated guy, clever enough to make quotations about the Alamo, the Custer disaster, and the assassination of President Lincoln.'

Jacob nodded. 'He sure doesn't need any history lessons, does he?'

'Those messages he sent you suggests he likes to joke, too – but he has a dark sense of humour. What's the word for that, Jake? I can't bring it readily to mind.'

Jacob raised his eyebrows and nodded. 'I think you mean macabre.'

Ed looked amazed. 'Mac . . . Mac what?'

'Macabre.'

'Well, bless my cotton socks and boots. I had no idea I was so well educated myself!'

Jacob smiled. 'You got the right sentiment even if you couldn't bring the word to mind, Ed. Anyway, dark is a good word, too, for what you wanted to say.'

Ed looked modestly pleased with himself. 'So, what are we going to do about it, Jake?'

'What I'm going to do about it is to ask my big second brain to look into the matter with some urgency.'

Ed's eyes widened with surprise. 'You mean you've two brains, Jake, a big one and a small one?'

Jacob grinned. 'Not exactly, Ed. I keep the small one in my head and the big one is in the head of my new assistant Pete.'

Ed sighed with relief. 'OK, I get it, but why do you always talk in riddles? This is a big deal we're talking here, Jake, a really big deal. You know there could be blood on the streets, your blood and my blood if we don't watch ourselves.'

'Or Killer Simms's blood,' Jacob said.

The three Merriweather children were walking down Main Street, with Pete a pace or two behind them. Pete was looking left and right like any other bodyguard, but he saw no sign of Killer Simms. Not that he expected to. After all, Simms was no fool, was he?

At that moment Jacob Junior stopped and waited for Pete to catch up.

'Excuse me, Mr Pete. I'd like to ask you a question.'

'Ask away, Mr Jacob.' Pete said with a smile.

'What's your other name, sir?'

'My name's Peter Savage.'

'Really!' Jacob Junior marvelled. 'So are you warlike, Mr Savage?'

'I've never thought about it much, Jacob. My father and mother and brother are all Savages. So I guess I'm stuck with it for the rest of my born days.'

'Wow!' Jacob Junior exclaimed. 'Peter Savage and Oscar Savage. That's really something, isn't it?'

Pete gave a wry smile. 'It's just about as important as your name – Merriweather.'

Jacob Junior pondered on that. 'You're right, Mr Savage. All names are strange, but some are stranger than others, aren't they?'

'I guess that must be true.'

'So, you're a Savage bodyguard now, aren't you, sir? Does that mean you're a dead shot?'

'Only in target practice, Jacob. So far I've never had the bad luck to have to shoot at a real person.'

Jacob Junior's eyes were keen with interest. 'I hear you carry a Smith and Wesson, sir.'

Pete nodded. He didn't care to discuss such matters in public, and Jacob Junior had a high, shrill voice. 'Why don't we walk faster and catch up on your two sisters?'

Jacob Junior laughed. 'They're both in love with you, Pete. You know that?'

Pete didn't reply. He was busy looking right and left and backwards and forwards. Of course, there was no sign of Killer Simms, but there were one or two other *hombres* who stared at them with interest.

'You know, Mr Savage, if I had a gun no badman would come near us. He wouldn't dare.'

'You're probably right, young sir, but right now all you have is me. So why don't you walk right on and talk to your sisters?'

'They're just silly girls, Mr Savage.'

That evening Jacob and Marie took their dinner with Cy Clavell and his wife in the restaurant of The Silversmith Hotel. Jacob had donned his best suit, and Marie looked resplendent in a brand new costume. Cy Clavell wore an expensive suit, and Amy Calvell had a sequin-covered costume that made her look like a radiant but dumb star. It was clear that the only person who spoke in that family was Cy Clavell himself.

He looked from Marie to Jacob. 'Well, well,' he said, 'I had no idea you two were married. When did you meet?'

'Some time back,' Jacob told him.

'That must have been a wonderful coincidence. And how many children do you have?'

He was looking directly at Jacob, but it was Marie who answered and told him about her three children. Cy Clavell nodded and smiled with approval, and his wife smiled modestly but said nothing.

'Do you have any children yourself?' Marie asked Amy directly. Amy blushed and looked down. 'Not as yet, Mrs Merriweather, not as yet.'

'That's all in the future,' Clavell said in a loud, over-confident tone.

They enjoyed a fine meal, in which Clavell outlined his plans for a huge emporium that would, according to him 'really make this sleepy town jump with prosperity'.

51

'It will bring business to you, too,' he promised.

After the meal, which lasted long into the evening, the ladies withdrew to Marie's private sitting room, and the men sat on, drinking whiskey and smoking Havana cigars. Jacob confined himself to the whiskey since he had never taken to smoking. The two men were sitting back in their soft seats when they heard what sounded like a disturbance outside on Main Street.

Trent Oldsmere appeared at the door, looking a little flustered. 'Excuse me, Mr Merriweather, but there's been a disturbance on the street.'

'What kind of disturbance?' Clavell demanded.

Oldsmere looked at Jacob. 'Shots were fired, sir, and Sheriff Mullins has been hit.'

Jacob leaped to his feet. 'Ed Mullins hit! Is it bad?'

'I don't know, sir. Doc Deacon is attending to him now.'

As soon as Jacob stepped out on to Main Street, he saw his friend Ed Mullins lying close to the sidewalk with Doctor Alex Deacon bending down beside him and several other folk gathered round. Ed's long-barrelled Colt lay beside him, and there was blood on the street.

Doctor Deacon looked up and said, 'Get back and give the man air.'

Jacob saw that Ed's eyes were open and he was gritting his teeth with pain. So at least he was alive!

Doctor Deacon looked directly at Jacob. 'I need to stop the bleeding and we'll need a stretcher to carry him to the hospital.'

Ed clenched his teeth and said, 'Help me up, Doctor, and I can walk.'

Doctor Deacon shook his head. 'That's impossible, Sheriff, if you want to stay alive. Just lie still while I bind you up.'

Ed lay back and closed his eyes and Doctor Deacon bound his wound, which was in his right leg. Doctor Deacon was a young man who had recently qualified, but he knew what he was doing, and soon he had managed to stop the bleeding. Two men had run up to the small hospital and brought a stretcher, and under the doctor's supervision they lifted Ed on to it. Ed almost passed out with the pain. He looked at Jacob. 'Tell my wife what happened to me, will you Jake?'

Jacob nodded. 'I'll go over right away.'

But there was no need to: Ed's wife Natalie appeared almost immediately. She came from old frontier stock and she didn't cry or scream: she just looked at her husband and grimaced. 'Who did this to you, Ed?'

Ed looked from her to Jacob. 'It was a man called Simms,' he said.

'Killer Simms,' Jacob said.

CHAPTER FOUR

Ed was more seriously wounded than was previously thought. The bullet had entered his thigh and nicked his right femur, which meant he would need to stay in hospital for at least a month or six weeks. But Doc Deacon didn't believe in patients lying in bed longer than necessary. So he soon got Ed walking on crutches up and down the ward, but a man on crutches isn't a whole lot of good as an officer of the law. So the town needed to find a deputy to act in his place, which wasn't easy since Ed had been sheriff for a number of years and he was a very popular and extremely dedicated officer.

After the shooting Jacob visited Ed on a daily basis. 'I've got your gun, Ed, but I guess you won't be needing it for a while,' he said the first time.

'Thanks, and I guess you're right,' Ed said, 'more's the pity.'

'So tell me exactly what happened, Ed.'

Ed sat on a chair beside his bed and nodded. 'Well, I guess I must tell you the truth, which is a little embarrassing for me. I was standing outside my office and that guy Simms came riding into town. Can you believe that? He actually rode into town cool and calm as a pool on a winter's night. So I drew my gun to make an arrest, but I wasn't quick enough for Simms. He loosed off a shot and hit me. I managed to fire my gun as I fell, but the bullet went wide. Simms fired another shot, but luckily that went wide too. So maybe I was lucky after all. The guy could have killed me stone dead!'

'Well, thank Jehosophat that you're still alive!' Jacob said.

'Well, whoever that guy Jehosophat is, I thank him too.' Ed gave a hoot of laughter, which made him wince with pain.

Without Ed, Jacob felt very much on his own as far as the law was concerned. A day after the shooting Cy Clavell turned up at the office. 'Is Mr Merriweather in?' he asked Dorothy.

'I'll look into his office and see, Mr Cavell.'

'Don't bother yourself, young lady. I'll walk right through myself.' He blustered his way into the office where Jacob and Oscar were deep in conversation.

'Good morning, Mr Merriweather. I'd appreciate a word with you,' Clavell said.

Jacob was already on his feet. 'I have five minutes in hand, Mr Clavell. What can I do for you?'

Oscar bowed to Clavell and left the room with scarcely a glance at Jacob. Clavell watched him closely. 'You have a fine young clerk there, Mr Merriweather.'

Jacob nodded in appreciation. 'A fine young man indeed, Mr Clavell. He's like a son to me. He's headed for a glowing career in the law.'

'That's a pity,' Clavell said. 'Otherwise I might be

inclined to take him on myself. I need reliable young men around me.'

Jacob thought he sounded like Julius Caesar in Shakespeare's famous play.

'Well now, Mr Merriweather. . . .' Clavell gathered his dark coat tails around him and sat down. 'After that unfortunate incident on Main Street last evening I've been turning things over in my mind.'

'Indeed, Mr Clavell. I guess we all have.'

Clavell nodded. 'That poor man, Mr Merriweather, that poor man Ed Mullins.'

'Doc Deacon tells me he's likely to make a full recovery in good time . . . I see him every day. He's a good friend.'

Clavell nodded sagely. 'I understand that kind of shooting is very rare in this town.'

'Things have calmed down a lot since the early days,' Jacob assured him. He wondered what Clavell was leading up to. He knew the man never wasted words on lost causes or idle projects.

'Bad for business, Mr Merriweather, bad for business' – Clavell gave Jacob a look of enquiry – 'And you have considerable business interests in this town, haven't you, what with your wife's hotel and the law firm?'

'Indeed I have, sir,' Jacob replied guardedly.

Clavell gave him a sudden slanting grin. 'You're a sly dog, Merriweather, a sly dog indeed.'

'I'm a lawyer, Mr Clavell.'

Clavell regarded him steadily for a moment. 'Your past, Mr Merriweather, your past.'

Jacob raised an eyebrow. 'We all have pasts, Mr Clavell, some darker and some lighter. We trail our past around with us for the rest of our lives, like a bag full of junk.'

'Pre-cisely!' Clavell snapped his fingers. 'And if you have something in that big bag, you shouldn't hide it under a bushel, as the saying goes. You should put it to good use and benefit from it.' He sat back in his chair with an air of complacency. 'I'm a business man, Mr Merriweather and I'm a strong believer in using my talents. That's how I got where I am today.'

Jacob gave him a quizzical look. 'Why don't you tell me what you're driving at, Mr Cavell? Plain talking has a deal to recommend it.'

'Well now, Mr Merriweather, you're damned right there, and I'd appreciate it if you called me Cy and I'll call you Jake. After that grand dinner your good lady provided I think we can count one another as friends, can't we?'

Jacob wasn't too sure about that. He wondered what was coming next, and he didn't have long to wait. Clavell leaned forward in his chair and nodded slowly. 'I've been reading up on your past, Jake. I've been reading up on your past . . . and it makes very interesting reading, too.'

Jacob folded his hands together and followed his dictum of saying nothing until he needed to. His spine tingled with anticipation, and he thought, 'Is this hombre threatening me?'

Clavell was showing his teeth in a grin. 'Don't worry, Jake, don't worry. That past we spoke about. Don't hide it, use it! That's my advice! You have nothing to be ashamed of, absolutely nothing. Blazon your past abroad. Tell the world your story.' He held up his hand to trace an imaginary headline: *Ex Gunman Becomes Distinguished Lawyer.* Maybe it should be *famous*, what do you think?

Jacob took a deep breath. 'OK, so you know something

about my past, but I don't quite see where you're going with this.'

Clavell showed his teeth in a grin that made him look like a neighing horse. 'Write a book, sir. Write a book. . . .'

Jacob raised an eyebrow. 'You don't by any chance know a young guy named Avril, do you?'

Clavell was still grinning. 'Of course I know Avril, and I knew it wouldn't take you long to tumble to that one, Jake. Sure, young Avril is the front man for my publishing business. He's a smart kid, a super smart kid. He's going right up the ladder to the top.'

Jacob said nothing for a moment. He didn't know whether to be surprised or outraged by this disclosure.

Clavell rose to his feet and gathered his tails around him. 'Well now, Jake, I won't bother you any longer this morning. I guess you must have many clients to see. This is a thriving law business. But think it over, think it over. I'll drop in and see you tomorrow.' He shook Jacob's hand abruptly and left the office.

Later that morning Oscar came into Jacob's office and Jacob told him about Cavell's proposal.

Oscar shrugged. 'Nothing surprises me, Boss. And maybe the man's right. You should publish a book. I myself would love to read your story, and it would enhance your reputation one hundred per cent.'

Jacob wasn't convinced about that. A profound sense of uncertainty had crept right into his bones and settled down like a hissing rattlesnake. He was too proud to discuss his concerns with Oscar in detail. So he went over to the hospital to talk things over with his good friend Ed Mullins. Mrs Mullins had just left her husband and he was walking up and down between the beds with his crutches, much to Doc Deacon's approval and the other patients' dismay.

'Ah, Jake,' Ed Mullins said. 'How good to see you, my friend.'

He sat on his bed and Jacob took the chair.

'There are a few things I want to talk over with you, Ed.'

'Good, good,' Ed said impatiently. 'I can't stand it here. The doc's kind enough, but those guys over there, all they do is grumble all day and fart and cuss and snore their heads off all night – that's their main occupation.' He laughed and winced, though his wound was healing pretty well.

'Now you're on the mend, Ed, I thought we could have a few words about Killer Simms.'

'Simms isn't worth a cuss. What he needs is a bullet through the heart.'

'That's what I want to talk to you about, Ed.'

Ed nodded towards the other end of the ward, which was just about within hearing distance. 'You see those two drunks down there?'

'I see them,' Jacob said. The two men in question were muttering to one another in low tones. Both had indefinable illnesses, and neither of them looked as though he would last much longer.

Ed lowered his voice. 'The one with the long grey beard is Lem. I heard him talking in his sleep last night, and you know what, he called out the name Simms.'

'Simms,' Jacob said quietly. He looked at the old wreck of a man and the man looked right back at him. 'What exactly did he say?' Jacob asked Ed.

'He just sat up in his cot and stared ahead of him as

though he could see Killer Simms himself standing in the doorway, and he shouted out, "Don't – don't do it, Simmy! Don't shoot, for God's sakes!" Then he just lay down and dozed off again.'

Jacob looked at the man and then at Ed. 'I think I'll just walk over and talk to the guy.' He got up and walked over to the man's bed. 'Excuse me, sir, I'd appreciate a word with you.'

The man looked at him sideways and immediately looked away again. 'Why, Mr Merriweather. I see you visiting the sheriff.'

'That's right.'

'Dang pity he was wounded like that.'

'Well, it could have been worse. He'll soon be out and well again. What happened to you?'

'Well, sir, I just pitched off the sidewalk and bust my shoulder and it still hurts something terrible, specially at nights – but the good doc is putting me together again so I can go home.'

'Where is home, sir?'

Lem looked at him in surprise. It was a long time since anyone had called him sir. 'Well, home is a long ways off from here, Mr Merriweather, a real long ways off. I need to hit the grub stacks afore I can go there. That's why I'm still here sitting in this god-damned bed.'

'Well, sir, maybe I can help you there.'

Lem narrowed his eyes with suspicion. 'How come, Mr Merriweather?'

'If you give me certain useful information I might just pay you up front.'

Lem narrowed his eyes even further. 'What information and what payment would that be, Mr Merriweather?'

'Let's just say enough to get you where you aim to go, and a little bit more to tide you over.'

Lem still looked highly suspicious. 'What information do you need?'

Jacob paused momentarily. 'Information about Simms.'

That made the hairs on the back of Lem's neck stand on end. 'Simms!' he said. 'What about Simms?'

'Simms,' Jacob repeated. 'The man who shot Ed Mullins.'

A look of terror leaped into Lem's eyes. 'I don't know anyone called Simms.'

'Then why do you call out to him in your sleep?'

'Who said I did?'

Jacob leaned forward. 'You sat up in your bed and shouted, "Don't shoot, Simmy! For God's sake don't shoot!"'

Lem looked all round the ward in amazement. 'That can't be! I never talk in my sleep!'

'Then how come those words came out of your mouth?'

Lem sat back in astonishment and thought things over. 'Well, yes, I did once meet a guy called Simms.'

'Killer Simms,' Jacob said. 'A killer with a price on his head.'

Lem shrugged. 'Well, yes, I might have known him, but I never rode with him.'

'Nobody's accusing you of riding with him or anything else, unless it's a crime to talk in your sleep.'

Lem relaxed a little. 'Well, I did know him once, Mr Merriweather. But I don't think I can help you now. It's way back.'

'That's too bad, Lem, because I think you might know more than you think.'

For the first time Lem looked Jacob straight in the eye. 'What is it you want of me, Mr Merriweather?'

Again Jacob paused. 'Just a piece of useful information, Lem. Nothing more.'

'What information?'

'If you tell where I can find Simms, I'll reward you, and you can go home where you belong.'

Lem puzzled over that for a moment. 'You don't know Simms. He's a real killer. If he knew I was talking to you right now I might as well be lying dead in a ditch. He's that sort of son of a bitch. He'd blow your head off as soon as look at you.'

'That's as maybe, Lem, and that's why the guy has to be stopped in his tracks before he kills any more people.'

'That may be so, Mr Merriweather, but I aim to stay alive a while longer, so I don't think I can help you.'

Jacob jingled the coins in his pocket. 'Simms will never know you gave me this information, and remember you'll be far away tucked tight as a tick in your own bed.' He opened his wallet and took out several dollar bills and placed them on a chair beside Lem's bed. Lem looked down at them with widening eyes. 'You must want him awful bad, Mr Merriweather.'

'Someone has to bring him to justice, Lem.' He placed several more dollar bills on the chair.

Lem looked down at them with a gleam in his eye. 'Well, I can't do much, Mr Merriweather, but if you'll hand me a piece of paper I'll write something down.'

Jacob opened his pocket book and tore out a sheet. Lem grabbed a pencil and scribbled something in large and ungainly handwriting with his tongue between his teeth. He then handed the paper to Jacob. 'There, Mr

Merriweather, that's the best I can do, but don't let anyone ever know I've given you this or my neck will be in the noose, or as good as.'

Jacob glanced at the paper and stowed it away in his pocket. He then peeled off some more dollar bills and handed them to Lem. 'Thank you, Lem. You've done a great service to the community.'

'Well, I sure hope you get him, Mr Merriweather. I sure do.'

At the other end of the ward Ed was waiting eagerly. 'Well, Jake, did you get anything?'

Jacob produced the paper and unfolded it. Inside it said 'Seehork'. Ed looked at it and grinned. 'Well, at least the guy knows his letters, even if he's a bit wobbly on his spelling.'

'So have you heard of somewhere called Sea Hawk?' Jacob asked him.

'Matter of fact I have,' Ed said.

'Sounds like some kind of eagle's nest,' Jacob speculated. 'D'you think that guy Lem is trying to make a fool out of me?'

'Well, he might be and he might not be, because there is a place called The Sea Hawk. It's a saloon right by the sea. And it has a real bad reputation.'

'Is it far from here?'

'Not so far. Quite an easy ride.'

'Worth a visit?' Jacob said.

Ed pulled a wry face. 'Not if you value your life, it isn't. So you think that might be where Killer Simms holes up?'

Jacob nodded. 'Could be. I won't know till I get there, will I?'

Ed moved restlessly on the bed. 'If you're going for Simms, I aim to come with you, Jake.'

Jacob shook his head. 'It will be some weeks before you can ride, let alone walk, and I can't wait that long.'

Ed held up his hand in protest, 'Why the hurry? Can't he wait until I'm fit and ready?'

Jacob shook his head. 'I don't think so, Ed. We don't know what Simms has planned, and I can't sit around and wait.'

'So, what do you figure to do?'

Jacob nodded. 'You tell me where The Sea Hawk is and I'll ride there and look the place over and take it from there.'

'Well, I don't know whether to call you a brave man or a damned fool,' Ed said.

'Let's just call it pest control,' Jacob replied.

That evening after the kids had gone to bed, Jacob and Marie were sitting over a welcoming fire, even though it was quite warm outside. Jacob had always been honest with Marie: he regarded it as being one of the corner stones of his marriage.

'I have to take a trip,' he told her.

Marie looked at him and smiled, and it was a smile of apprehension. 'I know about your trips,' she said. 'I guess you're taking that Colt .44 with you.'

Jacob knew better than to contradict Marie. 'I might be away for a day or two days, depending on the circumstances.'

'Well,' she said, 'just as long as you come back in one piece.'

'Oh, I aim to. I want to see those sweet kids of ours grow

up good and strong. That's what I'm going for.'

Marie nodded. 'I'd like to come with you.'

'I know you would, but you can't. You have to look after the kids and run the hotel.'

Marie looked thoughtful. 'What do you hope to achieve?'

Jacob paused. 'I need to get these people, whoever they are, out of our hair so we can live normally again.'

'You mean Simms?'

Jacob nodded. 'Simms, yes, but not only Simms. I have to find out once and for all who sent those poisonous messages, and straighten things out with them.'

Marie looked thoughtful. 'Straighten things out means shooting things out, I guess.'

'Not necessarily. Simms is an ugly *hombre* but he's a hired gun. I don't think he cares what happens either way. He just wants to kill and take his pay. He could have killed Ed and me, but he didn't. So if I get to confront him I might learn the truth about these poisonous *hombres*.'

Marie held her head on one side. 'So you're going alone?'

'I guess I have to. Young Pete Savage will be looking after the kids and Oscar will be taking care of the shop. And Ed is out of action, and will be for some weeks.'

'Well,' she said, 'you'd better say a prayer, because you're sure going to need it.'

Next morning Jacob called Oscar and his brother Pete into the office.

'Tomorrow I'll be out of the office,' he told them. 'I may be away for a day or two. I want you to take care of the office, Oscar, while I'm away. Tell the clients I've been

65

called away on unexpected business.' He switched to Pete. 'And I want you to look after the kids. Make sure nobody takes a shot at them. And don't take too much sass from young Jacob Junior.'

Pete gave his semi-military salute. 'Yes, Boss, and take good care yourself.'

Next day Jacob left early, but he wasn't wearing his sombre lawyer's outfit, he was wearing his range clothes. He had his gunbelt strapped to his side and he looked and felt like a different man. He left by the back way so that hardly anyone saw him. It was like the old days when he rode with his buddy Alphonso, who was now, he reminded himself, dead and gone.

Ed had given him directions to The Sea Hawk. So he took his time and followed the map in his head.

The Sea Hawk stood on a prominence close to the Pacific shore. A great place to take a break. There were no other buildings close by. Although it was painted up and smart to the eye, there was still something dark and brooding about it, like a toad squatting on a rock looking for a passing ant to lap up with its tongue and swallow.

Jacob noted there was a bell beside the door.

'Do I ring the bell?' he asked himself quietly.

'No, just open the door and walk right in,' he replied to himself. He dismounted and tethered his mount to the hitching post among the other mounts. No sign of Simms's horse. It was probably in the shelter at the side of the saloon.

He checked his Colt to make sure it was easy in its holster. Then he took a deep breath and pushed open the door. To the right was a table, where six card players sat. As the door was thrust open all heads turned and men sprang up as though the Angel of Death had stepped across the threshold.

Jacob swung quickly to the left where there was a long bar, behind which stood the bartender, a short balding man. Across the bar opposite him sat a man drinking from a tankard. It was Killer Simms.

As Simms swivelled on his stool towards the door he looked a little surprised, but not unduly so. Then in a flash his hand went to his gun and in less than the blink of an eye he was on his feet with his gun levelled at Jacob.

Then everything seemed to move in slow motion. The card players pushed up the table and ducked behind it, the cards flying into the air like a shower of falling leaves. The bartender disappeared abruptly behind the bar. Simms stood facing Jacob with his Colt in his hand. The bartender resurfaced from behind the bar with a sawn-off shotgun pointing in Jacob's direction. Jacob held his Colt level and trained on Simms.

There was a moment of absolute silence as though time itself was standing on its toes and holding its breath. Even the card players had frozen in various postures of terror. Jacob heard a clock ticking somewhere close by.

Then Simms gave a sinister chuckle. 'Well, well, well,' he said in a steady voice. 'So, Merriweather, you haven't lost your touch after all.'

Jacob shook his head but made no comment.

'I guess you've come to meet your maker,' Simms went on in the same drawling tone.

'I don't think he's ready for me yet,' Jacob said, while thinking the bartender with the sawn-off shotgun could be quite a problem.

'Listen, Simms,' Jacob said in as steady a voice as he could muster. 'I have no quarrel with you. It's the people who hired you I want.'

'Well now, Mister Merriweather, that's an interesting theory, because I'm the one here, and that's the best you can get.' He glanced briefly at the bartender and Jacob knew he was in for a fight and there was no escape. So he made a quick decision. He fired at Simms and then swung to fire at the bartender. Simms jerked back but managed to loose off with his Colt and the shot went so close to Jacob's head it took his hat off. The bartender discharged his sawn-off shotgun as he disappeared behind the bar with a crash of glasses and broken bottles.

Jacob turned to Simms again. The gunman was on his feet but his left shoulder was shattered. He tried to hold his gun steady so he could take another shot, but the pain was too much. He lurched towards the bar, tried to steady himself, then gradually slid to the floor.

Jacob kicked his gun away.

'I'm done for,' Simms groaned.

'I don't think so.' Jacob spoke between his teeth. 'That slug went right through your shoulder. If we get you bound up and stop the bleeding, I think you'll probably live.' He bent down and grabbed Simms by his uninjured arm and helped him to his feet. Simms stood gasping, his face as yellow as parchment. 'Why don't you put a bullet through my brain?' he muttered. 'I won't be any good to anyone with a smashed shoulder.'

Jacob smiled grimly. He was almost on the point of vomiting. 'You'll have to turn respectable,' he said. 'It could be the making of you, my friend.' He walked over and looked behind the bar at the bartender who was crouching there shitting his pants with fear.

'Anyone killed?' he croaked.

Jacob picked up the sawn-off shotgun and broke it across his knee. Then he smashed it against the bar so hard that a couple more bottles fell down and smashed.

The card players were now standing with their hands in the air.

'Don't shoot, Mister,' one of them pleaded.

'No need to worry,' Jacob said. 'We don't shoot innocent men and women, We just shoot to defend ourselves. Someone get a dressing and bind this guy up before he bleeds to death.'

One of the braver card players came forward. 'I have some medical training. Leave it to me.' He came forward and inspected the wound. 'Luckily the bullet passed right through. We need to staunch the flow of blood and disinfect the wound.' He turned to the bartender. 'Give me a bottle of your best whiskey.'

'Yes, sir,' the bartender croaked, 'right away, Doctor Wiggins.' He reached up and took down a bottle of bourbon whiskey.

'Bring me a clean cloth and something I can use as a pad,' the medic said. He might not have been a fully trained doctor, but he sure knew what he was doing.

'So you're a doctor,' Jacob said.

'I'm a dentist,' the man said as he bound up the wound and improvised a sling.

Though Simms was gritting his teeth against the pain he looked somewhat easier in his mind. 'Well, Doctor Wiggins, I guess I have to thank you for saving my life.'

'Well, Mr Simms, I'm glad I was on hand. Otherwise you

would be knocking on death's door. Keep that arm up and don't move about too much if you want to live a bit longer. It's a good thing he didn't aim for the heart, otherwise you'd be lying dead already.'

Jacob was in something of a quandary. Doc Wiggins had said Simms should be kept quiet in case he started bleeding again, but Jacob knew Simms was his best and only witness. 'Listen, Simms,' he said. 'Either I take you with me or we sit down right here and talk turkey.'

'This man isn't fit to ride a horse,' Wiggins said. 'If he bleeds again he's set to die.'

Jacob looked at Simms and shook his head. Then he turned to the bartender who was still shaking with fear. 'Has Simms got a room here?'

'Why, yes. Mr Simms stays here most of the time.' The bartender led the way through to a back room where there was a deal table and a few chairs and a bed.

'Why don't you sit down and rest for a while,' Jacob said to Simms. 'Do a little deep breathing while I ask you one or two questions.'

Simms sat on one of the chairs, which was none too comfortable, and rested his good arm on the table. Jacob had to concede, he looked close to dropping. Wiggins was shaking his head with concern. 'This man should be in the infirmary somewhere.'

Simms gritted his teeth. 'It's OK, Doc. Let the man ask his questions. It don't make no never mind to me.'

CHAPTER FIVE

'Ask any damn thing you want,' Simms growled. 'I'm done for, anyway.'

'You're not done for, Simms. In six weeks you'll be fit to go back to your old ways. Your right hand's still OK.'

Simms distorted his face in a grin. 'Except there's a price on my head, and you can claim it.'

Jacob shook his head. 'I had a price on my head one time, but I was lucky. I met a good woman and I studied for a law degree, and that helped to redeem me.'

Simms grimaced. His wound was giving him excruciating pain. Little beads of perspiration were breaking out all over his forehead. 'Well, Merriweather, you're still quick with a gun. I'll give you that.'

'You need to be steady, as well as quick with a gun. I just got lucky. If that bartender had held his nerve I'd have been splattered all over the saloon.'

'That's most likely so,' Simms agreed. 'But right now you're here, and that's all that matters, isn't it?'

Jacob grinned. 'Listen, Simms, I could have killed you for shooting up Sheriff Ed Mullins who happens to be a good friend of mine. But I'm glad I didn't. I don't want your blood on my hands, and I don't give a damn about that reward. You could have shot me when you rode through town the other day, but you fired over my head. Why would that be?'

Simms looked grim. 'I had to shoot Mullins because he was taking a bead on me. I'm real glad I didn't kill him. You get used to killing in this line of business. The first time it's difficult. After that it comes easier. But I don't enjoy it. You might call it a necessity.'

'Well, Ed's resting up in the town hospital right now Otherwise, he'd have been right here with me and that bartender might be lying dead behind the bar.'

'So what do you want of me now?' Simms asked him.

'Well, there are two things I want, Simms.'

Simms nodded. 'You sound just like my old school teacher before he gave us the birch.'

Jacob raised an eyebrow. 'So you actually went to school one time, Simms?'

Simms grinned. 'I was top of the class, but I figured life on the range was a whole lot more exciting.'

'That means you have some education, so you could get yourself some kind of honest respectable job if you had a mind to it.'

'Maybe, and maybe not. But what's the other question?'

'You can tell me who hired you, and why they're persecuting me and my family.'

Simms thought about that and Jacob could almost hear his brain ticking over. 'I don't know the details, Merriweather. I'm just a hired gun, you know. They pay the price and I do the job.'

'So who wrote those colourful messages I received?'

Simms shook his head and winced with the pain in his

shoulder. 'I don't write messages, Merriweather. I just do what I'm paid to do. It has been like that since the beginning of time, and it'll go on till the end of the time. Some men plan and plot. Other men act.'

'That may be so. But I don't think you were paid to kill me. I think you were paid to put the frighteners on me and my family.'

'I guess that's pretty close to the truth, Merriweather.'

'So, who paid you, and why, and what for? That's what I want to know.'

Simms shook his head. 'You ever heard the word revenge?'

'I've heard of it, Simms. Some great playwrights have written plays about it. The world is full of revengeful people, like you said.'

'That's what keeps me in my trade, Merriweather. You could call me the Grim Reaper.'

'So how about giving me a name?' Jacob asked him.

The wheels in Simm's brain started spinning furiously again. He was calculating what he should do. 'I can't give you a name. That's the professional code I follow, I guess – but if you throw a name at me and a few dollar bills I can give you a nod.'

'You're a hard man to fathom,' Jacob said. 'Tell me, how does the name Davidson chime in your head?'

Simms considered for a moment and then he nodded. 'That's a pretty loud bell, Merriweather. I hear it good and loud.'

'Well, thank you, Simms. Now we're getting somewhere just fine.'

Simms nodded again and then started to cough. 'Get me some water, man.' He went on coughing.

Jacob looked about for a cup of water, and when he turned again he was staring down the barrel of a revolver. And Simms was grinning at him.

'I said you were fast, but you're not quick thinking enough, Merriweather. I could blast you to Hell right now if I wanted to, and there isn't a damned thing you could do about it. Now raise your hands very slowly above your head if you don't mind.'

Jacob raised his hands.

'That's generous of you, Merriweather,' Simms said sarcastically.

Jacob was shaking inside, but he knew that showing fear would only add to his dilemma. 'What happens now?' he asked.

'That's for me to decide.' Simms gave a sinister chuckle. 'You know, your trouble is you're far too trusting, Merriweather. You can't trust a single soul in this world. Those who are too trusting die. That's a well known fact in my business. Kill or be killed, just like the beasts of the field. They neither sow nor reap, but they kill.'

Jacob kept himself very still. He glanced about looking for some way to get the drop on Simms, but there was nothing to hand.

'Have no fear,' Simms drawled. 'First off, I don't want to shoot you here in my own room and spill your blood all over Mr Gladwin's fine carpet. That would hardly be the polite thing to do to a host, would it?'

Jacob made no reply. Keep cool, he thought: a talking man is a whole lot better to deal with than a shooting man.

'No, that wouldn't do at all,' Simms said, and motioned with his revolver. 'Of course, I could always take you outside and shoot you against the wall.' He gave that sinister chuckle again. 'But there again, that would hardly be fair to Mr Gladwin, would it? Too many witnesses, anyway.' He motioned again with his revolver. 'Of course, there are other possibilities. Maybe you can think of a few yourself.'

Jacob shook his head.

'No, I thought not,' Simms said. 'You're a damned sight too smart for that. No wonder you took to the law. A man doesn't want to make suggestions about his own fate, does he? The executioner might be only too pleased to take him up on them.' He motioned again with his revolver. 'In any case, the man who hired me might not be too happy about that.'

'What does Davidson want?' Jacob asked.

'Ah!' Simms exclaimed. 'The dumb man speaks sense at last.' He waved his gun again. 'I'll tell you what he wants, Mr Merriweather. He wants your head on a platter, just like John the Baptist in the Holy Book. Did you ever read that fanciful yarn, Mr Merriweather?'

Jacob gave a faint smile. 'I read it at school, just like you,' he said.

'Indeed, indeed you did. And those Davidsons have special tastes. They not only want your head on a platter, they want to cut it off themselves.' He sighed. 'So, you know what I'm going to do? I'm going to do what I'm paid to do. I'm going take you right to them and say, "Here we are, sir and madam. You asked for Jacob Merriweather, and here he is. Do with him as you please." '

'OK, Simms. Let's just cut the cackle and mount up and ride, shall we?'

Simms looked faintly surprised. 'Good thinking, Mr Merriweather, good thinking. I admire a man who thinks about his future, even if it's somewhat bleak, and I knew you'd see reason at last. Let's mosey out to the corral, mount up and ride. Just walk ahead of me, if you please. I'll tell you which way to go. Please don't speak to any of the customers because I'll have my gun trained on you and I won't hesitate to use it if I have to.'

As Jacob walked through the saloon the bartender, who was also the owner A.P. Gladwin looked up enquiringly. 'You going somewhere, Mr Simms?'

'Me and Mr Merriweather are just taking a little ride together,' Simms told him. 'The country around here is so pretty at this time of the year.'

There was no sign of the dentist or the other poker players. They had vanished like smoke on a winter's evening. Simms and Jacob went out to get their horses. Jacob was thinking of ways he could distract Simms long enough to get the drop on him, but Simms had Jacob's gun tucked through his belt. So that could dangerous.

'Now, Mr Merriweather,' Simms drawled, 'I want you to bring up my horse, then we'll mount up and you can ride ahead of me. Like I said, I'd be happy to shoot you if you make a false move, but I don't want to. As a matter of fact as a fellow hired gun I'd prefer not to do that. We have our honour among hired guns, you know. So ride along as gentle as a grazing lamb and we'll both be fine.'

Jacob mounted up.

'Now, just ride on to your right, away from the sea,' Simms instructed. 'Can you feel the sea breeze on your face? Really refreshing, isn't it? Makes you feel it's good to be alive. Let's keep it that way, shall we?' He gave that sinister chuckle again.

They rode along the seashore for a mile or two and

then turned inland.

'How far do we go?' Jacob asked him.

Simms chuckled, 'Not too far. It'll maybe take an hour or less if we keep going steady as she goes.' Though he sounded cheerful enough, Jacob detected a weakening in his tone. Maybe his wound had opened again.

'You didn't tell me you were a naval man,' Jacob said over his shoulder.

'You don't need to be a sailor to know the language of the sea, but as it happens I was at sea for a time.'

'That's a good honest career,' Jacob said.

'Well, it might have been if I hadn't had difficulty with the skipper.'

'What kind of difficulty?'

'Trouble is, I had to shoot him. That's when I decided the sea was no life for me.'

'So was he the first man you killed?'

'Oh, I didn't kill him. I guess he must have survived. He's probably limping about on crutches to this very moment. But that's what gave me the idea of hiring myself out as a gunman, and it has paid good dividends so far.'

They rode on for perhaps another mile until they came to a creek that bubbled away towards the sea. Then Simms called out for Jacob to stop. Jacob turned his horse and reined in, and dismounted. Simms drew rein beside him and dismounted with some difficulty because of his wounded shoulder. Jacob saw the bandage was covered with new blood.

'Doc Wiggins was right,' Jacob said. 'Your wound has opened up again.' At that moment he could have lashed out at Simms and knocked him to the ground, but he didn't choose to.

'This man is a killer and there's a big price on his head,' he told himself. Yet still he did nothing.

Simms looked at him sideways. 'Listen, Merriweather, I think I've overreached myself. I should have listened to Doc Wiggins. I don't think I can go much further. Why don't you take your gun and shoot me between the eyes. I think I'm a goner, anyway.'

Jacob was in something of a quandary. 'Can I kill this man?' he asked himself. He reached out and took his Colt .44 from the man's belt.

'That's right, shoot me right between the eyes, like I said.' Simms grinned.

'I can't do that, Simms, and you know it.'

'That's right,' Simms grimaced. 'Too soft in the heart for action.'

Jacob holstered his gun. 'Sit down by the creek and rest, Simms. Then we'll decide the best thing to do.'

Simms lowered himself gently and sat down. Then he gradually keeled over and lay on his back. 'Look up at the sky, Merriweather, look up at the sky. You think there's anything up there?'

'Just clouds and stars and the moon,' Jacob said.

'What about angels? D'you think there are angels flying about up there?'

Jacob shrugged. 'I've never seen one myself.'

'Well, they won't take kindly to me, will they, not after all the bad things I've done?'

'Maybe they're more understanding than you think.'

The next second Simms had drifted off to sleep.

Jacob looked down at Simms' inert body and wondered what to do. Should he leave him to die out here alone and ride away? Should he turn and ride back to The Sea Hawk and tell the owner that his tenant was lying by the creek likely to die, in which case Doc Wiggins could ride out and save him? Or should he try to get him back to town and claim the reward on his head? As he was pondering over this, he looked up and saw two men riding towards him beside the creek. They rode right up to him and drew rein.

'Hi there,' said one of them in greeting.

Both men looked down at Simms's supine form. 'Has this man been wounded?' one of them asked.

'Looks close to death to me,' the other more sombre-looking hombre said.

'Do you boys know The Sea Hawk saloon?' Jacob asked them.

'We sure do,' the first man said.

'Bad reputation,' the glum hombre put in.

'Maybe you could ride back there and ask if Doc Wiggins could bring a flat-top buggy to carry this man back to the saloon so he could be attended to?'

'He'd never get there,' the glum hombre said. 'We move him he's set to die, anyways.'

At that point Simms's eyes flickered open. 'I'm not set to die yet, but I don't figure I can ride back either. Just ask Doc Wiggins to ride out and dress my wound and get me back.' Simms then closed his eyes and appeared to sleep again.

The glum *hombre* then came up with a solution. 'OK,' he said, 'I'll ride to The Sea Hawk. I guess I've seen this Doc Wiggins guy. If he's not dead drunk he'll probably come out here and we can carry this guy back. But right now he needs to rest. I see he totes a gun. I hope he won't shoot you guys.' He gave a grim hoot of laughter. Then he mounted his horse and rode on towards The Sea Hawk.

The other more cheerful guy squatted down beside Simms and said, 'Don't you worry none, sir. We'll make sure you get that wound bound up good and proper. But don't you move none.' He turned to Jacob. 'How did this happen, sir?'

Jacob said, 'Mr Simms got in the way of a bullet.'

'Simms!' the man said. 'Haven't I heard that name somewheres before?'

Simms eyes flickered open again. 'That's because I'm famous, sir. Some folk call me Killer Simms.'

The man grinned. 'I seen a poster about you, sir. I do believe there's a reward on your head.'

'Dead or alive,' Simms said. 'And now's your chance to claim it. You could share it between you.' He grimaced. 'Help me to sit up. If I can prop my back against a tree, it will be a deal more dignified when they come to lay me out.'

The man was now all of a dither. What sense of humour he possessed had deserted him completely. 'I don't think I can do that, Mr Simms.'

Simms looked at Jacob. 'Can you hoist me up, Merriweather?'

Jacob knelt down and dragged him by his right arm. Simms had turned a strange yellowish colour. There was a willow close by and Jacob managed to prop him up on it. Simms gritted his teeth.

'What a way to go,' he muttered. 'I thought I might die in a shoot-out, but instead it seems I'm like to die of a hole in the shoulder. I shouldn't have been such a damned fool.'

'Well, Simms, we're all fools in one way or another. Even the saints were fools at one time or another. It's just part of being human.'

'You're wiser than you think,' Simms told him.

'I'm not wise, Simms. I just know how to keep out of trouble.'

'Just take my hand if you will, Mr Merriweather and keep hold of it until Doc Wiggins arrives. He's an awful drunk. I hope he doesn't pull my teeth. I might not be beautiful, but I'll be a lot less pretty without them.'

It was quite a long time before Doc Wiggins arrived, but he did have a flat-top buggy, and several other men accompanied him. And he seemed to be comparatively sober, too.

'So you didn't get far, Simms,' he said sternly, 'I warned you not to travel, didn't I?'

'I guess I've been a damned fool, Doc.'

'Well, let's take a look at that wound.' He knelt down beside Simms and examined the wound. 'Well, you've certainly lost a hell of a lot blood, and that's for sure.'

'That's because I'm a bleeder, Doc.'

'You sure are, Simms, you sure are.'

Later that day Jacob rode straight back to The Silversmith Hotel, and when Marie saw him she burst into tears. 'Oh, Jacob, thank God you're back.'

'Well, it wasn't easy,' Jacob said, 'but it could have been a lot worse. One thing's for sure, you won't be seeing that guy Simms any time soon.'

'You mean he's in jail?'

'No, he's resting with a hole though his left shoulder.'

'You mean you shot him?'

Jacob shook his head. 'He tried to shoot me, so I had to shoot him.' He told her all that had happened at The Sea Hawk.

'So after you shot him he pulled a gun on you?'

'He had one hidden in his room.'

Jacob told her the whole story, and how Simms had a serious bleed and had to be taken back to The Sea Hawk on the flat-top buggy. 'So, Doc Wiggins saved his life twice over.' Jacob paused to think. 'Only trouble is, we're no further along with those Davidsons.'

'So it is the Davidsons who are sending those vengeful messages?' she said.

'Sure. Simms confirmed it. That's the only good that's come out of this mess so far.'

'What do we do now?' she asked.

'Well, I think I must go to the office and talk to my chief clerk and his brother Pete. Then I'll go over and see Ed and talk to him about the situation.'

When he walked into the office he found Oscar interviewing the somewhat portly figure of Cy Clavell. 'Ah, Mr Merriweather,' Clavell said. 'I hear you've been away catching evil men.' He laughed throatily. 'I'm sure glad you're back in one piece, sir. And by the way, this young man has been doing a great job talking to me about the law. I've thought of offering him a partnership in my business. He could look after the law side of things. What do you think of that, sir?'

Jacob looked at Oscar. 'Well, that's up to Oscar sir, but maybe he should qualify first.'

Cy Clavell showed his gold teeth in a smile. 'No need to worry about that, Mr Merriweather. I'll be happy to put him through law school myself.'

Oscar gave Jacob a subtle wink. 'That's mighty kind of you, Mr Clavell, but I think my place is right here at the moment.'

Clavell's smiled widened. 'Of course, I appreciate that. You have a wise head on your young shoulders, sir, and you have that special quality of loyalty.' He turned to Jacob. 'Have you thought over Mr Avril's proposal, Mr Merriweather?'

Jacob nodded. 'I'm still mulling it over, sir.'

'Good, good.' Clavell rubbed his hands together with apparent glee. 'By the way, sir, what happened to Killer Simms?'

'Well, sir, Mr Simms is out of action at the moment. He took a bullet in the left shoulder.'

'Did he now! So he's still in the land of the living?'

'Last time I saw him he was just about ticking over,' Jacob said.

Oscar looked at Jacob and smiled. 'That's sure good to hear, Boss.'

Clavell looked at each of them with keen interest. He was as shrewd as a squirrel collecting nuts against the winter. 'Well, I'll leave you two gentlemen to yourselves and go on my way. The builders are moving in next week to get my store up and running. We'll have a grand opening ceremony in a month or two if everything goes according to plan.'

After he'd left, Jacob told Oscar all that had happened at The Sea Hawk, and Oscar looked impressed but dubious. 'Well, you were lucky there, Boss. I guess that means you won't need Pete for escort duty with those kids of yours. He's got quite fond of them. So he might be a tad disappointed.'

'Well, I think we should leave things as they are for the moment. Those Davidsons might find another way of getting at the kids.'

'That's true,' Oscar admitted. 'So we'll need to think about what we're going to do to protect them.'

Jacob walked over to the hospital to enquire about his friend Ed Mullins. Ed was walking up and down the ward on crutches somewhat impatiently. There was no sign of any of the other patients, but Doctor Deacon was looking pleased with himself.

'How's the patient, Doctor?' Jacob asked him.

'He's doing fine,' Doctor Deacon said. 'As long as he doesn't overdo things, he should be back to normal in a few weeks. I'll leave you two gentlemen to put the world to rights.'

Ed Mullins sat himself down on his bed and put his crutches to one side. 'The sooner I can get rid of these damned crutches, the better,' he declared. 'So how are things going with you, my friend? I'm sure glad to see you're still in one piece.'

'Yes. And I'm glad about that too. It could have been a very different story. That guy Simms is as slippery as a rattlesnake and twice as venomous.' He told Ed the whole story, and Ed listened intently.

'You know your trouble, don't you, Jake? You still think you're as young as you were twenty years ago.'

'Well, I might not be young, but I outgunned Simms. He could have killed me, but he preferred to take me to those Davidsons. The strange thing is, I got to quite like the guy. We seemed to speak the same language.'

'Well, Jake, that's a damned fool thing to say. You keep

thinking that way, and you can say good-bye to life.'

Jacob felt inclined to give Ed a gentle tap on the arm, but he restrained himself because of Ed's injured leg. 'I've been turning things over in my mind and trying to figure out what to do next,' he said.

Ed nodded. 'It seems those Davidsons don't mean to leave you alone, do they?'

'I can't understand why they're so vengeful.'

'Well, one thing's for sure, we have to stop them in their tracks.'

'Yes, but how do we do that?'

They looked at each other for several seconds.

'Look,' Ed said. 'The only thing to do is to take the fight to them.'

Jacob nodded. 'I guess you're right, Ed.'

Ed paused. 'My leg's nearly healed. Wait a few days and I'll be ready to ride. Then we can go together.'

'This isn't your fight, Ed.'

Ed grinned. 'Oh, I think it is. That Killer Simms shot me up and I mean to get even with him, one way or the other. And if that means taking out those Davidsons, well, that's two birds with one stone, as I see it.'

CHAPTER SIX

A couple of days later another message was delivered to Jacob's office. It read: *Can you hear his blood crying from the ground, Jacob Merriweather?* Jacob read it through twice and then showed it to Oscar. Oscar read it and shook his head.

'Well, Boss, this is like the giant with many heads. As soon as you lop off one, another one grows to take its place. These people sure don't care for you too much, Boss.'

'Well, I'm sure glad Pete's still riding shotgun,' Jacob said. 'I hope he's getting in plenty of shooting practice with that Smith and Wesson of his.'

'He certainly is, Boss. Never misses a day.'

Ed Munnings had discharged himself from hospital immediately after Jacob had visited him, and now he was fully restored in his office with his crutches close at hand.

'Just as good as the hospital,' he boasted, 'though my wife's a damned sight better cook – but I didn't tell Doc Deacon that! Anyways, he hasn't got a wife to cook for him at the moment, so it's a whole lot better to be in the office. I might not be able to do much yet, but I can look over things and deputise guys to do the heavy stuff. I'd be happy to deputise young Pete Savage. I hear he's pretty handy with that shooting stick of his – not that I care too much for shooting myself. I like to work by persuasion and common sense, you know.'

'Well, I think these Davidsons are going to need a hell of a lot of persuading. They want my blood. What do you make of this?' Jacob pushed the message across Ed's desk.

Ed took it up and perused it, moving his lips as he read. Then he looked up. 'I think I should get myself some specs. My eyes ain't a heap of good for reading these days.' He tapped the paper with his finger. 'You know what this could mean, don't you, Jake? It could mean that guy Simms has died from his wound. Had you thought about that?'

Indeed, Jacob had thought about it. 'Only one way to find out. I must ride back to The Sea Hawk and talk to the owner and that dentist with the unlikely name of Wiggins.'

Ed agreed. 'Give me a couple of days and I'll ride up there with you.'

'If you're sure you'll be OK I'd appreciate that.'

Ed grinned. 'No need asking for Doc Deacon's say so, because he'll say it's a damned foolish notion.'

'And he's probably right at that!'

'Well, someone's got to make sure you don't put your head in a noose, Jake. You sure seem to have an uncanny inclination that way.'

But Fate is a wilful beast, and as usual she threw up something entirely unexpected. Next afternoon the Merriweather children were walking back from school escorted by Pete as usual. The two girls were slightly ahead, and Jacob Junior was in earnest conversation with Pete some paces behind.

'I want to learn how to shoot, Mr Savage. Do you think you could teach me?'

'Well, you'd have to ask your pa and ma's permission about that, young Jacob. There's no way I could do it without their say-so.'

Young Jacob gave a boyish smirk. 'My pa was a famous gunfighter way back. Did you know that?'

'I did hear something,' Pete acknowledged, unwilling to commit himself.

Young Jacob was still smirking to himself. 'Those old days must have been very exciting, Mr Savage. I wish I'd been there.'

'I think it would be a whole lot better if you concentrated on your school work and trained yourself to be a good lawyer like your pa, or even went into the hotel business like your ma.'

Young Jacob pulled a sceptical face. 'Well, Mr Savage, that would be OK if I had the brain for study, but the truth is I'm no good at school work, and I don't want to be, either. Sitting at a desk and talking to people would bore me out of my skull.' He gave a conspiratorial smile. 'And I don't think you like it much either, Mr Savage. I've heard you're interested in opening a theatre somewhere. I'm not sure what that is, but I hear it's a very exciting career.'

Pete was smiling to himself. 'Well, I can tell you one thing, young Jacob. It's a whole lot more exciting than shooting at people. Only the bad guys cheer when you shoot a man down, but if you're a good actor a whole lot of folk cheer and stamp their feet, and that's a deal better. It's what some folk call creativity.' As he spoke he had a faraway look in his eye, and that meant he was off his guard.

It was at that very moment that Fate struck home. Two riders came galloping past them at hell-neck speed. As they approached the girls, one of them stooped and grabbed Maisie by the arm and hoisted her off the ground. The other one swung round and trained his gun on Pete. Pete was half way to drawing his Smith and Wesson. 'You draw that gun and I'll shoot you dead!' the man growled.

The first rider had Maisie across his saddle, and he rode away with her kicking and screaming in his grasp.

As soon as Katie, the eldest sister, had realized what was happening she had lashed out at the kidnapper with fury, but the kidnapper had kicked at her and she now lay on her back on the sidewalk.

Pete and Jacob Junior rushed to her assistance, but she screamed at them, 'Go after Maisie – she's the one who needs help!' And she scrambled to her feet again without assistance. She had also lashed out at the second rider, but he had spurred away, and the last thing they saw of the two riders was dust and the distant figure of a wriggling Maisie.

'Damn it!' Peter shouted with his gun in the air.

'Damn it!' Jacob Junior repeated. 'They got my sister Maisie!'

Pete stepped out on to Main Street and holstered his gun. 'Well, I'll be damned, there wasn't a thing I could have done.'

'That's my fault, I kept you talking,' Jacob Junior admitted. 'What do we do now, Mr Savage?'

Pete was still staring into the distance where he could still see the retreating figures and Maisie across the saddle.

'We have to tell the boss immediately. This is a very bad situation, and I'm to blame.'

They didn't have far to go. Almost immediately, Jacob stepped out of the sheriff's office. Pete and Jacob Junior rushed over to him, followed immediately by Katie.

'They got Maisie!' she cried.

Pete was almost in tears. 'I couldn't stop them, Mr Merriweather. It was all so fast and I was afraid of shooting Maisie.'

For a moment Jacob said nothing. Then he turned and put a reassuring hand on Pete's arm. 'There wasn't a thing you could have done, my son,' he reassured him. 'Those men were intent on taking Maisie. You couldn't have known what they were about to do.'

'What do we do now?' Pete asked. 'Give me a horse and I'll ride after them.'

But he was talking to the air, as Jacob was already swinging on to his horse which Oscar had brought across Main Street. Oscar had seen everything that had happened and had acted immediately. He handed Jacob's gunbelt up to him, and Jacob grabbed it and galloped away in the direction the kidnappers had taken. It was almost impossible to read the signs in town. There were so many horses and buggies passing to and fro, but once he got out of town it was much easier going – in fact he could even smell the horses, and knew the riders must be no more than a mile ahead. So he pushed his mount as hard as he could. The whole town seemed to flash by as he rode, and folk looked up in amazement.

Beyond the town limits he pushed on steadily. There was a bend in the trail some way ahead, and Jacob knew that could be a danger point. As he approached, he saw a rider half concealed among the trees. So he drew rein and steadied to a trot, and then stopped.

The rider held his gun high, ready to shoot. 'OK, Merriweather, hold it right there.'

Jacob had his hand on his holster, but it would be difficult to draw and the other man could shoot him down before he tried. 'You got my daughter, Maisie,' he said hoarsely.

The man shook his head. 'No need to fret about Maisie,' he said, 'She's in safe hands, I can assure you. My brother's kind of fond of kids. So he won't harm a hair of her pretty head.'

'What does your brother want?'

The man shook his head. 'My brother doesn't want a single thing, only his pay.'

'Who's paying you?'

The man raised his eyebrows. 'You want to know a hell of a lot for a man in your position, don't you, Merriweather?'

'I want to know everything,' Jacob said. 'It's my daughter Maisie you're holding.'

'Purty name, Maisie,' the man said. 'If I had a daughter, I'd like to call her Maisie, just like that.'

Jacob felt himself beginning to blaze with fury, but said to himself: 'Keep yourself calm. Don't let the man see you're rattled.'

'So what happened to Simms?' he asked the man.

'Well,' the man answered, 'that's a sad story. Fact is someone shot him in the arm, but he wouldn't lie down and rest. He just went right on as usual, and . . .' The man shrugged – 'you can guess what happened next – he died, and nobody could do a thing to save him.' He gave a bark of laughter. 'What a way for a killer to go! Don't you agree, Mr Merriweather? It's a real cruel world. No justice to be found anywhere.'

Jacob shook his head. 'Listen,' he said. 'I don't know who you are, but tell me this: what do they want and what happens next?'

There was a pause. 'What happens next depends on you, Mr Merriweather. Everything is in your hands, including the life of that little girl of yours.'

Jacob winced inwardly. 'OK. Maybe you'll explain.'

The man nodded. 'Sure, I'll explain. This is the deal. They've got Maisie, but they don't want Maisie, they want you.'

Jacob felt a freezing numbness creeping through his limbs. 'So what do I do?'

'You wait, sir.'

'So what do I wait for?'

'You wait for them to decide.'

'And when will that be?'

The man chuckled. 'You'll get a message telling you where to meet them, and then they'll hand over Maisie in exchange for you.'

'How soon will that be?'

'Soon, sir, very soon. A matter of days, I guess.' He rode forwards with his six-shooter levelled at Jacob – though he knew that Jacob wouldn't make a move against him in case Maisie came to harm. The man showed his carious teeth in a grin. 'Now, why don't you just turn your horse around and ride back to town, Mr Merriweather? There ain't much good you can do out here, either for you or Maisie.'

'How do I know Maisie's going to be safe?'

The man put his head on one side. 'You don't know

that, Mr Merriweather. Nobody does. The only thing we can do is to put our trust in the gods – and they're not too reliable, so I hear.' He jigged his horse to the right. 'And please don't try to follow me, Mr Merriweather, because it won't do you or Maisie any good.'

He pulled his mount round to the right and rode away, chuckling to himself.

Jacob watched him until the last moment. Then he turned his horse and rode back to town. He didn't hurry because he needed time to think, to work things out. He knew Maisie was a quiet, introspective girl, but she had her wild side. Of course, she would struggle and fight, and those vicious people might be tempted to harm her. On the other hand, holding her prisoner could be a hell of a problem for them. It would be like caging a wildcat.

As he rode back he saw Pete Savage and his brother Oscar riding towards him.

'So, you've turned back, Boss!' Oscar said.

'Only thing I could do,' Jacob said, and he told them all that had happened.

'So what will you do now?' Pete asked him.

'I wait,' Jacob told him. 'That is, unless someone a lot smarter than me can come up with a better idea.'

The two brothers exchanged glances, but didn't reply. Pete was still on the point of sobbing, but he managed to hold himself in. 'I'd do anything to rescue that young lady . . . anything at all. This is all my fault,' he said.

'It isn't your fault,' Jacob reassured him, and Oscar put a comforting hand on his brother's arm.

Back in town everything was in state of turmoil, especially in The Silversmith Hotel. Marie had a face like chalk and

Katie was sobbing. Young Jacob was furious with himself as much as anybody else.

'I'm to blame for this!' he shouted, 'I should have kept my eyes on Main Street. Instead, I kept Mr Savage talking when he should have been protecting the girls.'

Ed Munnings and his wife were in the main lounge and Ed was almost grinding his molars with fury. 'What in hell's name are we going to do about this?' he shouted.

'I think we have to wait until these people send through a message,' Jacob said. 'They want me, not Maisie. I have to make sure Maisie's safe, and I hope she has enough savvy to look after herself.'

'So we're stuck out on a limb,' Ed said.

'I guess so, until we receive that message,' Jacob said.

None of the Merriweather family slept much that night. Jacob could hear Katie sobbing and walking up and down in her room, and he heard Jacob Junior swearing and kicking out at the furniture. When Jacob did drop off momentarily he had vivid dreams in which his younger daughter was struggling with horrible green and yellow demons eight feet high!

Next morning at breakfast they all sat round the kitchen table with faces like lard. Marie was doing her best to keep calm and serve breakfast as usual, but her hands were shaking and she could hardly hold the bowls.

'I can't eat anything,' Katie said, pushing her bowl away.

Jacob Junior, on the other hand, was ravenous. He attacked his food as though he was devouring his worst enemy.

'I'm not going to school,' Katie declared vehemently.

'I think you must,' Marie said. 'We must all carry on as

usual. I'm sure your father agrees.'

Jacob did agree.

After Katie and Jacob Junior had gone to school, escorted as usual by a crestfallen Pete Savage, Jacob and Marie sat at the table and tried to talk things through.

'Why are these people so downright revengeful?' Marie asked in bewilderment.

'I don't know the answer to that,' Jacob said, 'but I guess I'll soon find out.'

As they were conferring, Jacob's assistant Dorothy appeared, and she looked decidedly down in the mouth – in fact she was close to tears, too. 'Excuse me, Mr Merriweather, this message came through for you. I thought you should have it straightaway, so I brought it straight from the office.'

'Thank you, Dorothy.' Jacob took the message and read it aloud: *The bell is tolling, Jacob Merriweather, and it's tolling for you. If you want to see your daughter Maisie alive again, come with my agent when he calls, and come alone. We don't want any accidents, do we, Jacob?*

Jacob looked at Dorothy and shook his head. 'Thanks for bringing the message, Dorothy. Go right back to the office and tell Oscar and the clients I'm going on a journey and I might be some time.'

'Yes, Mr Merriweather.' Dorothy curtsied and went out sobbing.

Before Jacob could say another word, Cy Clavell appeared. 'Well, well,' he said, 'I've heard all about it. In fact, I saw what happened yesterday. Now what do we aim to do about this? That poor girl must be scared right out of her wits!' He turned to Marie. 'Oh, I'm sorry, Marie. I didn't want to make matters worse. Quite unforgivable of me.' Then he turned back to Jacob. 'Is there anything I can do to help? This is a dreadful situation!'

Jacob looked at him and smiled. 'Well, Cy, I really appreciate your concern, but there isn't a thing you can do. Right now, we have to move cautiously and do exactly as these people say. I don't want my daughter's life in more danger than it is.' He showed Clavell the message and the man read it through with growing frustration and annoyance. 'These people, whoever they are, are like poisonous rattlesnakes. What will you do?'

Jacob glanced at Marie. 'For some reason they want to get back at me, and I shall do what they say. The most important thing is to get Maisie free. Nothing else matters to me.'

Later that morning a boy walked into the hotel. 'Mr Merriweather!' he called. 'There's a man outside and he's calling for you. He says you have to get on your horse and go with him right away.'

Jacob was on his feet immediately. He turned to Marie and said, 'Don't worry, my love. One way or another I'm going to get Maisie out of this.'

'I want you *both* out of it,' Marie said.

Jacob nodded. 'All you need to do is talk to Ed. He'll know what to do.' He gave her a last kiss and went to the door to retrieve his horse.

Out in Main Street the gunman he'd spoken to the day before was sitting on his horse waiting. Jacob swung on to his horse. 'OK,' he said, 'lead the way and we'll take it from here.'

As they rode to the end of town people came out of their houses to stare. It was almost like a stately procession.

Jacob and the gunman rode side by side almost like partners.

Jacob turned to the gunman. 'I don't know where we're going, but it's a damned fool's errand. These Davidson people can't possibly get away with it, you know.'

The gunman chuckled. 'Well, Mr Merriweather, you may be right, but I can tell you this, they don't like you one little bit. They think you killed their brother and they want to get even with you and I don't think you can blame them for that.'

'Well, I might have killed a few people in my time but I sure didn't kill Jack Davidson.'

The gunman shrugged. 'Tell them that. You'll soon have the chance. But I don't think they're in a mood to listen to you. I think they want to break you, Merriweather. They're not too keen about the way you killed Simms, either. Everyone thought he wore invisible armour. Just shows you what fools we humans are, doesn't it?' He chuckled. 'By the way, that girl Maisie of yours is a real wildcat. It must run in the family.'

'Well, as long as she's alive and unharmed, that's all that matters,' Jacob said.

'Oh,' the man said. 'She's more than alive. She's like a mountain lion defending her young. She nearly scratched my brother's eyes out.'

As they rode on Jacob took careful note of the route they followed. He knew they weren't headed in the direction of The Sea Hawk. He also knew that his friends back in town wouldn't be too far behind. 'You know, my friend,' he said, 'this whole business is an unholy mess, and it isn't going to end well.'

The man gave that throaty chuckle again. 'I know that,

and you know that, but do *they* know that? That's the big question.'

Jacob looked at him squarely. 'How did you get into this business, my friend?'

Now the man gave a bark of laughter. 'I got into it the same way you did, Mr Merriweather. My brother and me just rode West and decided we liked the outdoor life and the wide open spaces. So we hired ourselves out as gun-slingers. The best thing we've ever done, you know. We'll never be rich, but we're a damned sight richer than we could be serving behind a store counter or sitting at a desk with a pen behind our ears.'

'Except you have a good chance of lying on Boot Hill in the near future,' Jacob suggested.

'Well, we all end up there sooner or later,' the man said philosophically. 'So that's no never mind to me.'

'I guess you could have enlisted in the army,' Jacob said. 'Then you might have died young but they'd have given you a medal.'

'Dead men don't give a damn about medals,' the man replied.

'When we get there, how do I know Maisie will be safe?' Jacob demanded.

The man grinned. 'Well, Mr Merriweather, I guess you'll have to trust me on that. The deal is this, when we get there, I give a signal and my brother brings the girl out and we have a fair exchange. You go with my brother and Maisie comes with me. And then I take her back where she belongs.' He looked quizzically at Jacob. 'I don't know what happens to you after that, but I'll keep my fingers crossed and pray to the gods of mercy to spare you, wherever they happen to be.'

They rode on in silence for maybe another mile. There was a faint trail, but clearly not many people rode that way. Eventually they came within sight of a cabin.

'Well, here we are, Mr Merriweather, and all you can do now is to pray to those gods I spoke about. If we meet again I hope it's in better circumstances, and not at the end of a gun.' He shook his head with apparent regret, then he gave a high-pitched whistle.

The door of the cabin opened cautiously and a man emerged pushing a girl ahead of him – and the girl was Maisie Merriweather. When she saw her father she ran forwards towards him, shouting, 'Pa! Pa! You're here.' Then she ran into his arms.

Jacob felt a huge wave of relief. 'Thank God you're safe!' he said. The next moment he was swinging her round with delight and relief.

'OK,' the second gunman said. 'Now you come with me. Your daughter can ride your horse because I don't think you're going to need it any time soon . . . if ever.' And he laughed, just like his brother.

They watched Maisie and the gunman ride on but Maisie kept looking back with regret. Jacob wondered what would happen to her.

'What's going to happen to my pa?' Maisie asked the gunman.

The gunman sighed. 'I don't know the answer to that, Missie. It's in the lap of the gods.'

'What does that mean?' Maisie demanded.

'It means nobody knows.'

After a short while the gunman reined in. 'Why don't you just ride on, Miss Maisie, I think I have to turn back here, because I have other things to do.'

He swung round and headed back the way they'd come, and he was chuckling like a jay bird.

Maisie was an accomplished rider. She'd been in the saddle since she was four years old, so she rode on towards town. It was some distance, but she took her time. Her mind was racing ahead. What could she do to save her father? And why were they so eager to take him prisoner?

While she was thinking she heard the sound of horses approaching and in a moment scores of people swung round the bend towards her. They were led by Sheriff Ed Mullins. As soon as he saw her he spurred his horse on towards her. But it was her mother she fixed her eyes on. And soon they rode up to one another.

'Thank God you're safe!' Marie shouted.

CHAPTER SEVEN

'So what happens now?' Jacob asked the gunman.

'Well, we just ride on, Mr Merriweather.'

'But I don't have a horse.'

'No need to fret about that. A hoss will be provided. It might not be the best hoss in the world, but it's good enough to carry you to where you're going. Just walk right on and you'll find the hoss in the barn, and don't think about any tricks, cos if you do I'll be obliged to shoot you, and that won't be a lot of good to anyone, and the Davidsons won't be any too happy about it either.'

Jacob found the horse saddled and waiting for him in the barn. It was a real crow-bait horse, well past its best, but it had a good eye. Jacob ran his hand down its nose and chucked it under the chin, and it seemed to appreciate the gesture.

'I hope you're in a friendly mood because you might have to carry me to hell and back,' Jacob told it. The beast tossed its head as if it understood.

'I'm not sure about carrying you back, Mr Merriweather,' the gunman said pessimistically, 'but I guess he can carry you pretty well to hell. So mount up and we'll ride on just as soon as my brother catches up with us.'

Jacob mounted the crow-bait horse, and they waited.

'So you two are brothers?' Jacob said.

'Sure thing,' the gunman said. 'Blood brothers. I'm Chuck Clarkson and he's Jim Clarkson. Jim's three years older than me. You could say he led me astray, but it wasn't difficult – I was already halfway there.' He chuckled deep in his throat. 'You could say we're a partnership in crime.' He sounded boastful and increasingly relaxed.

'Keep him talking,' Jacob thought. 'The more he relaxes, the more he lowers his guard.'

'Where are you from, Chuck?' he asked.

Chuck raised his head. 'We're originally from Philadelphia, the City of Brotherly Love. I guess you might have heard of it.'

'Well, it didn't teach you much, did it, my son?'

'Well, Mr Merriweather, I'll tell you this. It taught us quite a lot. I don't hate any man. We just do what we're paid to do, just like you did when you were in the gun-slinging trade.'

Jacob nodded. 'That was way back. You're a little out of date, my son. Didn't anyone ever tell you those days are long passed?'

'As a matter of fact, you're wrong there, Mr Merriweather. We'll never be out of date, not as long as there are humankind on this plant.'

'Yes, and there'll always be rich guys with gold and silver coming out of their ears to hire you to kill those they have a grudge against.'

'Well, we seem to agree on that, Mr Merriweather – but here comes brother Jim.'

Jim Clarkson rode into the clearing in something of a hurry, but he didn't dismount and he looked sort of nervous. 'Well, Chuck, I see you're both mounted up and ready, so I guess we should ride on in case we're being followed.'

'We'll be followed, right enough,' Jacob said. 'My people aren't fools, you know. You're the fools for staying in this business.'

'That may be so, Mr Merriweather, but they must be savvy enough to know that if they get too close we might have to shoot you, in which case they might just as well go home and sit by the fire and toast their toes.'

Both brothers then had a good chuckling session, which suited Jacob just fine.

The two brothers then rode close on each side of Jacob so they couldn't be picked off by anyone following. They were so close they were practically knee to knee with him, Jim Clarkson on his left and Chuck Clarkson on his right.

'How far is it?' Jacob asked them.

'How far is it to Babylon?' Jim Clarkson laughed.

'Can I get there by candlelight?' Chuck crowed in response.

Jacob considered his position. Should he wait until his friend Ed Mullins caught up with them, as surely he would, or should he make his own move as soon as he saw the chance? The brothers were both right-handed, which meant that both had their pistols in holsters on their right hips. So which was his best bet?

It didn't take him long to work it out. In fact it was now or never. He reached out quickly and gave Chuck Clarkson a mighty heave which sent him flying to his right and out of the saddle. His horse sprang forward and bolted as Chuck disappeared over its side.

'What the hell!' cried Jim Clarkson. But he should have saved his breath because the next second he felt the full force of Jacob's fist on the side of his head, followed by a mighty shove which sent him out of the saddle and on to the ground. It was a long way down, and when he hit the ground it knocked the wind out of his chest completely, and as his head hit the ground he was knocked unconscious.

Jacob might have been old, but he still had his strength, and his elderly horse served him well. He leaped out of the saddle just in time to confront Chuck Clarkson, who was attempting to draw his gun. There was no time for refinements, so Jacob just kicked him hard in the face. There was a dull plop and the gunman fell back with a gasp. Jacob kicked him again, and then reached down to relieve him of his gun. Then he turned and yelled, and the horses bolted.

Jim Clarkson had managed to sit up. He shook his head and drew his gun.

'Throw that gun down!' Jacob shouted hoarsely.

It was too late. Jim Clarkson raised the gun and was about to fire.

Jacob ran forwards as if to kick the gun away, but Clarkson fired. The slug came so close to Jacob's head he felt it singe the hair above his right ear. He acted on impulse and fired. Clarkson reared back and lay on his back with his mouth wide open. He gasped twice and lay still, staring up at nothing with an expression of amazement on his face.

Jacob turned quickly towards Chuck Clarkson. But a familiar voice said, 'OK. Just get yourself up on your feet and don't make a false move or you'll be dead meat.' It was Ed Mullins speaking, and he had his Buntline Special trained on Chuck Clarkson. Clarkson got up slowly and he looked equally amazed. 'My God,' he said, 'you killed my brother Jim!'

Jacob shook his head. Yes, he had killed Jim Clarkson, and he didn't feel in the least triumphant. In fact he felt as though he was about to throw up.

Ed Mullins reached out and gripped his arm. 'You had to do it, Jake. It was him or you.'

Jacob shook his head again. He felt meaner and more wretched than he had ever felt before. He had to admit to himself that he had actually quite liked the man he had killed.

'Well, you haven't lost your touch, Mr Merriweather,' someone said, and it was Pete Savage.

The two men had been following closely – there was no way they would have lost track of the Clarksons and their buddy Jacob Merriweather.

Chuck Clarkson was staring down at his dead brother. 'Will somebody close his eyes? If he keeps staring at me like that I shall go completely crazy!'

Ed knelt down and closed the dead man's eyes.

'What do we do now?' he asked Jacob.

Jacob shook his head. 'There's only one thing we can do. We ride on until we come face to face with these Davidson people.'

Pete Savage offered to round up the horses. It seemed that when he was in the circus business he had been around horses a great deal and had learned how to talk to them. He was in fact a remarkably accomplished young man.

The question now was, what would they do with Jim Clarkson's body?

'I'm not leaving my brother's body here to be eaten by coyotes and buzzards,' Chuck Clarkson said. 'I want him buried properly according to the rites of the church. After all, he was only doing his job. I don't think he meant to kill you, Mr Merriweather.'

'Maybe not,' Jacob said, 'but the fact is he took a shot at me and missed by a hair's breadth, and that's why he's lying there now.'

Chuck Clarkson had to accept that as a reasonable argument.

Rounding up the horses proved to be quite easy, and Pete soon reappeared with them in tow.

'What happens now?' he asked.

'Well, Mr Savage,' Ed said. 'You're probably the youngest here, and Mr Merriweather and me think you should carry the body back to town and ask the funeral director to keep it on ice till this fiasco is over with. Then he can give the man a respectable burial.'

'If that's gonna happen,' Chuck Clarkson said, 'I think I should go with him. After all, it's my brother we're talking about here.'

Jacob shook his head. 'That all sounds nice and neat and civilized, except for one thing, Clarkson, and that is you're the only one who can lead us to the place where those Davidsons are holed up.'

Clarkson looked doubtful. 'I'm afraid I can't do that, Mr Merriweather.'

'I think you have to,' Ed said.

Clarkson shook his head. 'You can't get blood out of a stone, sir.'

Ed peered at him. 'You don't look like a stone to me, Clarkson.'

Chuck Clarkson shook his head again. 'You don't understand, Sheriff. What I mean is, I can't take you there because I don't know where they are. The only one who knew that was my brother, and he's dead.'

'And what the hell does that mean?' Ed Mullins asked him.

'It means exactly what I told you,' Chuck Clarkson replied. 'I never knew where the Davidsons were holed up. That's because they hired my brother Jim, and I went along with him. Jim always did the business end of things and we shared the job. That's all I can tell you.'

'Well, Clarkson,' Ed said. 'That's a good story. The only trouble is, I don't believe a word of it.'

Clarkson shrugged. 'You might not believe it, but it's true.'

Ed looked at Jacob, and Jacob pulled a sceptical face.

'OK,' Ed said. 'In that case I guess we should all head back to town. We take your brother to the funeral parlour, and the funeral director lays him out with his hands across his chest like he was a good Christian gentleman.' He turned to Chuck Clarkson. 'And I lock you up in the town calaboose until you decide you do know the way to the Davidsons. Then you can lead us right up to their doorstep.'

Clarkson shook his head. 'Like I said, you can't get blood out of a stone. I can't lead you there, because I don't know where they are.' For the first time he looked a little off balance.

'OK,' Ed said. 'So we turn our horses and head back to town.'

They lifted up Jim Clarkson's body and laid it across his horse's saddle. The horse turned its head as though it wondered why its master was mounting up in such a strange fashion, but then looked ahead as if it was thinking it was a no-never-mind situation in the world of horse sense.

Then they all rode back in the direction of town.

When they reached town, folk abandoned their work and came running out on to Main Street to stare at the strange procession – the dead body of a man lying across the back of a horse, and a group of men carrying guns, including the sheriff. As they passed The Silversmith Hotel several of the guests emerged, among them Marie, who gasped with astonishment. She didn't say anything, but Jacob knew what she was thinking well enough: she had been sick with worry about him.

Where Cy Clavell's new building was being erected Clavell himself emerged. He looked delighted, shouted that he wanted to take photographs with his new camera – but the party rode on to the funeral parlour where they lifted Jim Clarkson's body down with care and carried it into the hall of rest with due reverence.

'Keep my brother safe, sir,' Chuck Clarkson instructed the funeral director.

'Don't concern yourself unduly, sir. They're all the same to us here. They're just human beings who've passed on. We don't enquire about their past, be it good or bad, and they have no future in this world, anyway.' He spoke in a sombre, not to say morbid tone of voice, in keeping with his profession.

'And now it's time to lock you up in the town cala- boose,' Ed Mullins said to Chuck Clarkson. 'It might not be quite up to the standard of The Silversmith Hotel, but I think you'll find the food is good enough to keep body and soul together while you stay.'

Chuck Clarkson pulled a wry face and made no comment.

Jacob rode straight back to the hotel where the hotel manager Trent Oldsmere greeted him warmly. 'So glad you're safe, Mr Merriweather. Mrs Merriweather has worried sick about you.'

Jacob didn't need to be told that. The next moment, Marie appeared and she was weeping with joy. 'What happened?' she asked.

Jacob gave an account of the events that had taken place without undue elaboration.

'Who killed that man?' Marie asked.

Jacob had to admit that he had shot Jim Clarkson. 'And I'm sorry for it. He tried to shoot me. So I had no choice.'

'Well,' Marie said, 'you look quite tuckered out. Your clothes are all soiled, and you look like you've been rolling in prairie dust.'

Jacob looked down at his coat, which was indeed ripped in places and covered with dust.

'Clothes are one thing,' he said. 'But people are another. I think I shall hit the tub and then take a long, long sleep.'

'I think you deserve it,' Marie agreed.

Jacob luxuriated in the tub for so long he nearly dropped off to sleep. He climbed out, dried himself and fell into bed. He slept so long that when he woke up it was quite dark and Marie was lying beside him. So he turned over and went right off to sleep again.

He woke to the sound of cock crow and the savoury smell of frying ham. Marie stood at the door with a tray.

'I thought you deserved breakfast in bed,' she said with a smile.

Jacob swung his legs out of bed and stood up. 'Thanks,' he said, 'but you know I don't eat breakfast in bed. It gives me indigestion.'

Marie smiled. 'Very well, I'll take it downstairs.'

Jacob felt mean. 'Give it to me. I'll bring it down.' He took the tray from her and laid it on a side table.

'By the way,' she said, 'young Mr Pete Savage is downstairs waiting to talk to you. It seems quite urgent.'

'OK. I'll be down immediately.' He dressed in clean clothes and took the tray downstairs.

Young Pete Savage was sitting at the table waiting for him. 'Good morning, Boss,' he piped up cheerfully. 'That breakfast smells mighty appetizing.'

'Have some ham,' Jacob said, passing him a spare plate.

'Thank you, Boss, I can't resist it.'

'Don't they feed you up at home?' Marie said.

Pete smiled. 'Well, yes they do. Ma's an excellent cook, but this smells quite delicious.'

Marie poured him a generous mugful of coffee.

'So,' Jacob said, 'you wanted to talk to me?'

'Indeed, sir. I've been thinking a lot since yesterday.'

Jacob smiled. 'Haven't we all, my son. And what conclusions have you come up with?'

Pete paused for a moment. 'That guy Clarkson might know where the Davidsons are holed up, and he might not. But I don't think it matters a damn either way, because it seems to me we can work it out without him.'

Jacob nodded. 'You're a genius, Pete. I dreamed the

same thing last night, and you've brought my dream back to me.'

'So what are your conclusions, Boss?'

Jacob took a long swig of his strong coffee. 'I think that guy Fergus Walsh who came to see me about getting rid of his wife wasn't Walsh at all, but Davidson. That tale about wanting to get rid of his wife was just a ruse to lure me into his trap.'

Pete Savage clapped his hands with glee. 'You got it, Boss! The guy wanted to lure you in so he could discredit you. He wants to drive you out of town.'

Jacob nodded. 'I think he wants a lot more than that. He wants my head on a platter like the king and John the Baptist.'

Pete winced. 'What a gruesome picture you paint, Boss. He thinks you killed his cousin, or whatever relation he is, and he wants to see you dead.'

'The question is, what do we do about it?' Jacob pondered more to himself than to Pete.

'Well, Boss, in my opinion there's only one thing we can do. We have to take the fight right to them.'

'That sounds like good thinking,' Jacob said. 'The only thing wrong with it is, we don't know where they are, do we?'

Pete stood up and touched the side of his nose with his right forefinger: 'Leave it to me, Boss. I'm working on it.' He drank the last of his coffee and went to the door. Then he turned. 'By the way, Boss, that was the best breakfast I've had in a thousand years! Not that I've lived for a thousand years.' He gave a broad wink and disappeared laughing.

*

But before they could proceed any further another completely unexpected thing occurred. Chuck Clarkson broke out of the town calaboose. The young man who had been assigned to take him his meals had become somewhat too trusting, and he and Chuck had struck up quite an easy-going relationship. When he entered the prison building the young man in question, whose name was Phil Stermer, called out, 'Good morning, Mr Clarkson. I've brought your grub stakes, and it smells good enough to eat!'

Chuck Clarkson appeared to be asleep in his cot, but he opened his eyes and pulled himself up on to his feet. 'What is it, Phil, bread and scrape?'

'Oh no, Mr Clarkson, something far better than that. You've got the best toasted rye bread and some kind of spread, and even an egg. It should keep you going for a while.'

'Well, thank you for that,' Clarkson said in quite a friendly tone.

Phil Stermer put the tray down on a table outside the cell, then took down the key and unlocked the door and entered the cell. Then he turned to retrieve the tray – which was a big mistake. In no more than a second Chuck Clarkson had him by the neck in a stranglehold. Phil Stermer attempted to throw him off but Clarkson was strong and desperate, and he held on until Stermer went limp. Then Clarkson released him and Stermer slid to the floor,

Clarkson gave him a hearty kick and stamped on him hard, but there was no response. The breakfast delivery man was already dead.

Clarkson looked down at him with cold indifference. The effort of throttling the man had made him quite breathless. But he couldn't afford to waste any time at all: the sheriff might come into the jail house at any moment. So he looked round the room quickly and saw a Winchester hanging on the rack.

'Ah, that's just what I'm looking for,' he muttered to himself. He went to the desk and slid open a drawer, and sure enough, there was a box of Winchester cartridges. So he levered the Winchester open and loaded it. Then he went to the door and looked out cautiously. 'What I need is a horse,' he said to himself.

At that moment either Providence or the devil intervened. A man rode up to the sheriff's office and dismounted. Clarkson pushed open the door and covered the man with the Winchester. 'Give me that horse,' he demanded, 'and stand still in case I have to shoot you down!'

The man didn't need any second bidding. He put his hands up and backed away. 'Don't shoot, sir. You can have the horse.'

Clarkson swung up into the saddle, and the man made no move to stop him. He was, in fact, a simple farmer, and he had no grudge against any man or woman.

Clarkson pulled the horse round with the intention of riding out of town, but at that moment Sheriff Ed Munnings appeared. He drew his long-barrelled Colt and aimed it at Clarkson. 'Get off that horse or I fire!' he commanded. But Chuck Clarkson was in no mood to argue with anyone. He levelled the Winchester at Ed Mullins and fired. Ed fired as he went down, but the shot went wide.

'You asked for that, you son of a bitch!' Clarkson shouted as he turned the horse and rode towards the end of town as fast as he could.

Right at that moment Jacob Merriweather and Pete Savage came running across Main Street. Jacob looked at the rapidly retreating figure of Chuck Clarkson.

'He stole my horse and shot the sheriff!' the farmer said in amazement.

Jacob bent over Ed Mullins, and to his relief the sheriff's eyes flickered open. But there was a large stain of blood spreading across the front of his shirt. 'Am I dead?' Mullins croaked out.

'Lie still, Ed,' Jacob said. He knew that if Ed tried to move he might die. The shell seemed to have entered his chest on his left side, but at least he could still breathe and talk.

Doc Deacon arrived almost immediately. He knelt down and examined Ed's wound. 'First thing we have to do is stop the bleeding,' he said. 'Lie absolutely still, Sheriff. As soon as the bleeding stops I must get you into hospital.'

'Thank you, Doc,' Ed muttered, and then he closed his eyes and lost consciousness.

A great wailing of women came from the prison, and a woman rushed out on to the street.

'They've killed Phil Stermer!' she cried.

Jacob went into the prison building and saw several women bending over the stricken man. 'They killed my man!' Mrs Stermer sobbed.

Jacob looked down at the dead man, whose eyes were still bulging with horror, his tongue purple and thrust out in his last gasp.

'He was just delivering the man's breakfast, too,' a woman wailed. 'That beast deserves to roast in hell!'

'And he probably will!' another woman said.

Jacob went out on to Main Street and saw two men carrying Ed on a stretcher. Mrs Mullins was walking beside the stretcher on one side and Doc Deacon was walking on the other side. Pete Savage was on the sidewalk waiting for Jacob.

'Ed's been hurt pretty bad, Boss. The doc says the bullet's still lodged in his back, but luckily it missed his spine and it's close to the surface. So the doc should be able to dig it out without too much trouble. But they don't know whether he's likely to pull through or not. And as to that guy Clarkson, we're on our own, Boss. So what do we do now?'

Jacob looked towards the end of Main Street and saw that things were pretty much the same as usual. Chuck Clarkson and the farmer's horse had vanished completely, and there wasn't even a cloud of dust.

Jacob shrugged. 'What we do, my son, is we go ahead and find out where those ornery people are holed up. Then we go in for the kill.'

CHAPTER EIGHT

'Where do we begin, Boss?' Pete Savage asked.

Jacob smiled grimly. 'Well, my son, we begin at the beginning. You carry on with your enquiries and I continue with mine. And my research starts at The Sea Hawk Saloon where that unfortunate gunman came to grief.'

Pete nodded. 'So when do we start, Boss?'

'The day after tomorrow.' Jacob looked Pete in the eye. 'But I should warn you, my son, that it will be very dangerous. I want things laid out fair and square. So you'd better tell your pa and ma where we're going in case one of us gets injured.'

'You mean killed, Boss,' Pete said. 'Let's lay out our cards. No good beating about the bush, is there, Boss?'

Jacob smiled. 'Well, my son, I don't know where you're going but wherever it is you'll get there pretty well on time.'

'Unless I get *injured*, eh, Boss.' He gave Jacob a broad wink. 'My ma and pa know what's going on, anyway. I keep them pretty well informed, and my ma insists on knowing. She's a pretty insistent woman. Needs to be with a husband like our pa. He offered to come with us but he's too much of a rummy. He'd shoot someone in the back without meaning to.'

'Sounds like a real liability,' Jacob said.

'Well, you know what it is, Boss. A man gets sort of frustrated doing nothing. Thinks he isn't worth a cent. So he turns to drink.'

'That sounds real sad,' Jacob admitted. 'We must do what we can to help him.'

Jacob then went to Doc Deacon's hospital to see how his friend Ed Mullins was getting on. Doc Deacon shook his head glumly. 'The sheriff's asleep. I had to sedate him.'

'Is he going to pull through?' Jacob asked.

The doctor shook his head again. 'I'm afraid it's too early to say. I did manage to extract the bullet, but I need to keep him quiet. He's been through a hell of a lot lately.'

Jacob nodded in agreement.

Doc Deacon frowned. 'The only person who can see him at the moment is Mrs Mullins. Later, perhaps. . . .' He shook his head again. 'There's been too much killing recently.'

Jacob had to agree with that, too.

Then Jacob spoke to his chief clerk Oscar. Of course, Oscar knew what had happened, how Chuck Clarkson had killed the man bringing his breakfast, and had wounded the sheriff, possibly fatally.

'This is real scary,' Oscar said. 'You and my brother Pete will be putting yourselves at great risk. I hope you know that.'

'We're already in danger. Those Dickinsons won't let go until they've killed us, or driven us into the desert like sacrificial lambs. So we have to act in self defence.'

'So what d'you want me to do, Boss?'

'I want you to mind the shop, as before. Like I said, when this is all over, I shall put you through law school and offer you a partnership. And you can bring your pa in tomorrow. Maybe he can't do much, but he can do a few errands as long as he lays off the bottle.'

'Well, that's mighty generous of you, Boss. Pa will appreciate that.'

Back at the hotel Jacob discussed the whole situation with his wife. Marie was a highly intelligent woman, and she understood what was happening very well.

'If only I could come with you,' she said.

'Well, we know that's impossible, don't we?' Jacob said.

'And that young man, Peter Savage. He might be rash and get you both into deep trouble. And don't ruin another suit,' she added with a laugh.

'I shan't be wearing my lawyer's gear,' Jacob said. 'I shall be wearing those old clothes I wore when we first met.'

Marie smiled. 'Well, try not to roll in the dust, anyway.'

The following morning Jacob and Pete dressed themselves in range clothes, and Jacob tooled them both up with Winchester carbines. But just before they set out, a man with greying hair appeared.

'Good morning, sir. My name's Savage. I'm Pete and Oscar's pa and I'm offering my services in a good cause.'

Jacob looked him up and down and decided he wasn't as far gone in drink as Pete had suggested. 'You mean you want to come with us, Mr Savage?'

Jeremiah Savage gave Jacob a grin which revealed a severe lack of teeth. 'Don't take no notice of those boys of mine. I used to be a sharpshooter, so I know which end of a gun is which. Just give me a gun and a good horse and I

118

think you might find me useful.'

Jacob nodded. 'Well, Mr Sharp Shooter Jeremiah Savage, I'll be glad to have you along, just as long as you don't shoot yourself in the foot.'

Jeremiah Savage showed his blackened stumps again in a smile. 'You won't regret it, Mr Merriweather. I can assure you on that.'

Jacob arranged to meet Pete and Jeremiah at the bend in the trail some way out of town. Jacob was there first, and he scouted around to make sure there was nobody skulking in the cottonwood trees. He was still among the trees when the other two showed up.

'Where's the boss?' Pete said to his father.

'He'll be around,' his father said philosophically.

Jacob jigged his horse forwards and Jeremiah swung round to face him.

'Hold your fire!' Jacob said. 'And save your ammunition for the bad guys.'

'Can't be too careful,' Jeremiah replied. He and Pete looked like a couple of real hillbillies out on a duck shoot.

'What happens now, Boss?' Pete asked.

'Well, we ride on to The Sea Hawk,' Jacob told him. 'It isn't too far.'

'I know The Sea Hawk,' Jeremiah piped up, 'but it ain't the place you'd take your bride on your honeymoon. It's real rundown.'

'Well, that's where we're headed,' Jacob said. 'When we get there, you wait and I ride ahead. We don't want to take unnecessary risks, do we?'

'Well,' Pete said, 'I guess you won't find anybody there. Those Dickinsons are way too smart, and if you ask me, Chuck Clarkson will be keeping a low profile after what happened in town.'

'You could be right,' Jacob said, 'but there again, you could be wrong. We have to be ready for anything.'

After quite a long ride they came to the coast, and there was The Sea Hawk. It stood a little apart from a cluster of other unpretentious buildings.

'There she is,' Jeremiah said. 'Just as I remember it, only a whole lot worse. So what's our next move, Mr Merriweather?'

'I go in first and you follow close behind. Pete, I want you to face the door so that nobody can come in and shoot us in the back.'

Pete nodded. 'OK, Boss, that sounds like good sense.'

Jacob turned to Jeremiah. 'And don't shoot unless I tell you. We don't want unnecessary bloodshed, do we?'

Jeremiah growled, but said nothing discernible.

They dismounted and hitched their horses to the hitching rail. Jacob pushed open the door. Every face in the saloon turned to look at him. It was almost like a re-run of the time before, except, of course, there was no gunman Killer Simms whom Jacob had killed. The same faces stared at him from the card table, including that of the dentist Doc Wiggins who had treated Simms unsuccessfully. The barman stared at Jacob for a moment and then reached for a weapon. It wasn't the shotgun since Jacob had smashed it.

Jacob held up his empty hand. 'No need for shooting, sir. We've just come in for refreshments.'

The barman gave a faint smile. 'OK. What can I get you? Whiskey, beer?'

'We'll take three beers,' Jacob told him.

The barman poured the drinks and pushed them across the counter.

'What's this piss?' Jeremiah asked after taking a sip.

'The best we've got, sir,' the barman said.

The card players were still staring apprehensively in Jacob's direction. Wiggins the dentist stood up and came towards Jacob. 'Well, sir, I don't know what you're looking for, but you won't find it here.'

Jacob nodded. 'You're probably right, Doc, but you never know what you're going to find unless you look, do you?'

Wiggins grimaced. 'That's true enough, sir.'

Jacob turned to the barman. 'The name Clarkson mean anything to you?'

The barman shrugged. 'I've heard tell of the brothers Clarkson, but I don't recall they've ever shown up here.'

Jacob nodded. 'Does the name Dickinson ring a bell in your head?'

'I don't hear bells, Mr Merriweather. If I did, I'd know I was going plumb loco.'

The men at the card table laughed, and a man sitting apart in a corner away from the bar, stood up. 'I know the Clarksons, Jim and Chuck. I saw them a while back, but not recently.'

Jacob nodded again. 'You might not have seen them but they were working for the Dickinsons. One of them got shot and the other one broke out of the town jail and killed the man bringing him his breakfast and wounded the sheriff. That's a real case of biting the hand that feeds you, don't you think?'

'I guess so,' the man agreed. 'But I can't help you with Chuck Clarkson. That's way out of my territory. So one of them is dead and the other broke out of the town jail? So which one is dead?'

Jacob gritted his teeth. 'Jim Clarkson is dead. He had an unfortunate collision with one of my bullets. He took a pop at me. So I had to defend myself. Otherwise I might have been lying on the slab instead of him.'

That gave rise to more ragged laughter. Jacob realized that he had a somewhat grim reputation, which didn't altogether please him.

'So what about the Dickinsons?' he asked.

Now the barman laughed. 'Those rich dudes wouldn't come in here, Mr Merriweather. They're far too grand.'

Doc Wiggins spoke up again. 'I know the name. Wasn't a Dickinson shot down in his own ranch house by a masked gunman some twenty or so years back? I remember reading about it in the news-sheets.'

'I believe that is so,' Jacob agreed.

'And nobody found out who did it, even to this day,' Doc Wiggins continued.

'You're remarkably well informed, sir,' Jacob said.

Jeremiah gave a sinister chuckle. 'You might not remember me, Doc, but I have good reason to remember you. I came in here once and you offered to fix my teeth before they all fell out.'

Doc Wiggins grinned – his own teeth were in remarkably good order. 'Looks like I gave you good advice, sir. But by the look of your teeth you didn't take it.'

The card players and the man in the corner all hooted with laughter. Jeremiah showed his black stumps in a grin. 'You think you could patch me up before I lose them altogether?'

Doc Wiggins shook his head. 'Difficult to tell, sir. You'd

need to come to my office for an inspection. Otherwise you might have to practise chewing on your gums, which is not good for the digestion.'

There was more laughter, in which Jeremiah Savage joined. 'You might sell me some false gnashers, Doc.'

Wiggins nodded. 'They don't come cheap, sir.'

Everyone cackled with laughter again, which lightened the tone considerably.

But the next instant they heard the pop, pop, pop of gunfire outside, and Pete Savage appeared in the doorway. 'Someone's shooting, Boss!' he shouted.

Jacob and Jeremiah turned abruptly and left the saloon without so much as a word with the bartender or the card players.

'Take care!' Jacob warned Jeremiah Savage. But Jeremiah needed no warning. He might have been a sharpshooter in the army looking for a target to show up.

At that moment another shot came in from the hill behind the saloon.

Jeremiah pointing up at the hill. 'They're up there!' he said. 'I saw the flash!' He levelled his Winchester and fired a shot. 'Can't hope to hit them from here, but they can't hope to hit us at that range, either.'

'So what do we do?' Pete asked his father.

Jeremiah didn't hesitate. 'We smoke them out!' he said. Jacob realized that, although Jeremiah was a drunk, with the right incentive he was a vigorous and active guy who knew well enough what to do in an emergency. Jeremiah turned to Jacob. 'Keep their heads down while I go up there and smoke them out, like the stinking rats they are!' He swung on to his horse and spurred towards the hill.

'I'm going with him,' Jacob said. 'You keep their heads

down, my son! When I signal, you come up and join us.'

'OK, Boss, but take care. The old man is riding right into the jaws of hell, if you ask me.'

'I think your old man has a lot of grit,' Jacob said. As he swung on to his horse another shot came in, and Pete fired back immediately. 'Take that, you ornery bastard!' he shouted.

Jacob saw that Jeremiah was riding towards the hill by a roundabout route, so he headed straight for the hill to deflect the gunman's attention – but there was no more fire. He rode to the top of the ridge and waited for Jeremiah to join him, which was in no more than a minute or two.

'Vanished like the morning mist,' Jeremiah said breathlessly. 'I didn't think he'd hang around waiting for us to pop at him.'

'I reckon that was Clarkson,' Jacob said. 'Which means he knew darned well where we were.'

'Yes, sir,' Jeremiah agreed. 'You know what that means, Mr Merriweather?'

Jacob shook his head. 'I guess it means Clarkson knew perfectly well where we were headed, and he's probably hand in glove with those men in The Sea Hawk.'

'So do we go back, or do we go on?' Jeremiah asked him.

'We go on,' Jacob said. 'We can sort out that nest of rattlesnakes later.' He turned to the edge of the ridge and waved Pete on, and Pete joined them in less than a minute.

'What's happening, Boss?' he asked.

'We're riding on, boy,' his father said. 'That guy won't be far ahead, and it should be easy enough to pick up his tracks.'

Young Pete looked at Jacob with raised eyebrows. 'Whatever you say, Boss.'

They rode on cautiously, pausing occasionally to read the signs. Jacob was struck by Jeremiah's keenness. He was like a terrier eager for the hunt, and seemed an entirely different man from the character his sons had described.

'Take care!' Jacob warned, 'He might be leading us into a trap.'

'Which means we spread out,' said Jeremiah. 'I follow the signs while you boys ride on either side in case we have to flush him out.'

'Right, Boss,' Pete said, with a tinge of irony on the word boss.

Jeremiah rode on, stopping from time to time to look at the signs. From the way he operated he might have been a native. After a while he paused and held up his hand, and then motioned the other two to close in. When they came together he spoke almost in a whisper. 'This guy, whoever he is, is no amateur. He knows we're following him, and in fact he wants us to follow him.' He pointed to the tracks. 'Lookee there, where he's turned. My guess is he's circling round to get behind us. Luckily his hoss decided to let loose his horse apples just at this point, almost as if he wanted to show us the way!'

Jacob turned in the saddle and looked up through the trees where there was a slight bluff. 'My guess is he's up there waiting for us to get within range to shoot at us.'

'There could be more than one of them,' Pete suggested. 'Why don't we circle round so we can box them in?'

Jacob considered for a moment. 'Maybe you're right, my son. There could be a whole bunch of them, and they might want us to do just what you've suggested. Then they can pick us off one by one like heads popping up on a shooting range.'

'Except,' Pete said, 'they want to take you alive, Boss.'

'Maybe I should let them take me. Then you boys can ride home in peace and settle down to your proper jobs,' Jacob said.

Jeremiah shook his head. 'You know we can't do that, Mr Merriweather. We're in this up to our necks.' He looked at his son. 'You should go back, Peter. After all, you're the next generation and that means a lot to an old geek like me.'

Pete grinned. 'I can't do that, Pa, and you know it.'

'So' – Jeremiah shook his grizzled head – 'we're in something of a fix here. So what do we do?'

Pete's eyes flashed with intelligence. 'Well, we could go right back to The Sea Hawk and await developments.'

'How would that help?' Jeremiah asked.

'It would give these poisonous rattlesnakes something to fasten their teeth into, wouldn't it?' Pete said.

Jacob paused to consider. 'I think we should go right back to town. If those yellow-bellied bastards want me enough they'll have to come and get me. You boys have done enough, and I'm mighty grateful for that.'

Jeremiah and his son exchanged glances.

'You sure that's what you want, Boss?' Pete said.

Jacob nodded. 'Yes, that's what I want. As soon as we find out where those Dickinsons are holed up, it'll be a different story. So you'd better put your special thinking headgear on, Pete, to find out where the Dickinsons run their business. If they're as stinking rich as we think they might be, it shouldn't be so difficult, should it?'

'No, Boss.' Pete looked quite pleased. 'I guess I'm more able using my brains than my gun, anyway.'

His father looked somewhat glum. 'Well, that includes me out,' he said, 'just as I was getting my second wind in this business, too.'

'No need to fret over that, Jeremiah,' Jacob said, 'because I'm going to offer you permanent employment, anyway.'

Jeremiah perked up immediately. 'Doing what, Mr Merriweather?' he asked.

Jacob grinned. 'Just guarding my back, Mr Savage. If those boys of yours had told me about your skills I'd have taken you on earlier, but you know what kids are like. They always sell the older generation down the river. It has been so from the beginning of time I guess, and it will go on until the end of the world.'

Pete and his father laughed. 'Your boss has a good head on his shoulders,' Jeremiah said

So they turned away from the bluff and started back to town.

Back at the hotel, Jacob told Marie everything that had occurred.

'So we're back to where we started,' she said.

'Not exactly,' Jacob replied. 'There's another man in my outfit and he's a lot better than I could have expected.' He told her about Jeremiah Savage. 'I don't know how he learned, but he seems to be almost as skilled as a native. So I've taken him on on a permanent basis.'

Maisie smiled. 'You're as soft as a whole pat of butter, Mr Merriweather.'

'Well,' he grinned, 'it sometimes pays to be soft and

malleable. Bending is better than breaking.'

He then walked over to the hospital to see how his friend Ed Mullins the sheriff was doing. Doc Deacon reported that Ed was alive but very weak, and that it was still touch and go with him. He advised Jacob not to over-excite him.

Ed was actually sitting up in bed, though he looked as weak as a sick puppy.

'How are you, my friend?' Jacob asked him.

'Well,' Ed said, 'at least I'm still in the land of the living. I guess they'd have told me if I'd passed on.' He gave a grunt of laughter, which turned into a coughing fit.

'Take it easy,' Jacob said.

Ed grimaced. 'All they're feeding me is slops. I long to get a good solid steak between my teeth. '

'I guess the doc knows what's best for you,' Jacob said.

'I think my belly knows better. But give me the lowdown on everything that's happened since I got shot.'

Jacob told him the story, keeping it as low key as possi-ble. Ed listened intently, nodding occasionally with approval or disapproval. 'Sounds like that Jeremiah guy is manna from heaven. A pity I couldn't have been with you. But right now I feel I might be lying here till kingdom come, and that's some stretch.' He chuckled again and gri-maced.

'You have to just do what the doc says and get yourself back in shape.'

'Can't I just take a swig of rye now and again to lift my spirits?'

'Learn to read,' Jacob advised. 'They say reading's good for the soul.'

'I think my soul's taken a long flight to fairyland,' Ed

said with a grin.

Jacob left the hospital and stood on the sidewalk looking left and right. The town was fairly quiet except for Cy Clavell's building works, which were proceeding apace. Jacob walked across Main Street with a sense of deflation. It seemed that this business with the Dickinsons was going nowhere at all.

In the office Dorothy greeted him with apparent pleasure. 'Good day, Mr Merriweather. How are things with you, sir? '

'Thanks for asking, Dorothy. Things could be a lot better, but they could be a lot worse, too. So I can't complain. How are things with you?'

'Things are just fine, Mr Merriweather. Oscar and I are getting married, but I guess you knew that already, didn't you?'

'Well, Dorothy, I'm very happy for you both. When and where will you be tying the joyful knot?'

'Well, we haven't fixed a date yet, but it'll be very soon.' She was blushing slightly under her tan. 'I hope you'll be there, sir. Oscar wanted you to be best man, but that goes to his brother Pete.'

'As it should,' Jacob said. 'I guess you've met the family.'

Dorothy gave him an arch smile. 'They invited me over to supper. Mr Savage is a sweety and Mrs Savage . . .' She raised her pretty eyebrows . . . 'Well, Mrs Savage is a force to be reckoned with. Nothing happens without her say-so.'

Jacob grinned. 'Maybe you should talk to Mrs Merriweather. She knows a thing or two about handling difficult men, and she's probably just as good with difficult women, too!'

*

Next day Pete Savage came into the office. 'Wine!' he shouted waving a bottle.

'Whiskey!' Jacob shouted in reply.

Pete laughed and pointed a finger at Jacob. 'That's pretty quick, Boss!'

'Now you can tell me what you're talking about.'

'Sure thing, Boss. Those Davidsons own a whole wine-growing area near the coast. I'm surprised I didn't think of that before.'

'Well, well.' Jacob twiddled his thumbs. 'Are you sure?'

'As sure as can be.' Pete held up the bottle of red wine. The label said, 'Ruby Red'. 'Read the small print at the bottom, Boss.'

Jacob held it up to the light and squinted at it closely. 'Dee Vinery,' he said.

'That's right, Boss. "Dee" means "Davidson", and I should have thought of that before. Stupid of me.' He hit himself on the front of the head.

Jacob shook his head. 'So you're sure?'

'Sure as I can be, Boss.' Pete looked pleased with himself, almost smug. 'And I've been asking around, too. Dee Vineries are close to the coast not too far from here. They open their bar every day and you can sample their wines. I guess my pa's been there, and they probably carried him out dead drunk.'

Jacob brought his hand down firmly on his desk. 'I don't think you should speak of your pa like that! He has a lot of potential, as you should have seen for yourself on our trip. Basically he's a very sound man.'

Pete had the grace to look somewhat shamefaced. 'Thank you – you're right, Boss. I should be more respectful.'

Jacob nodded. 'The question is, what do we do now?'

'Well now, I think a little drunken orgy might be in order, Boss.'

CHAPTER NINE

'Dee Vinery!' Marie exclaimed. 'Surely not!' She picked up the bottle and examined the label. 'We stock Dee Wines. Our clients seem to favour them. I think young Peter Savage must be slightly off beam.'

Jacob put his finger on the map. 'It's right there.'

Marie looked closely at the map. 'Well, that's not far from here. But I think this must be a joke, Jacob.'

'A joke in extremely bad taste, since men have died and my friend Ed Mullins is lying in hospital hanging on to life by a thread.'

'So what do you mean to do about it?'

Jacob shrugged. 'I'm going to do just what young Pete Savage suggests.'

'Like what?'

'I'm going to ride up to the vinery and take a drink or two.'

'Well, you'd better restrict it to two and not go alone.'

Jacob grinned. 'Otherwise the Big Bad Wolf will get me, eh?'

Marie almost stamped her foot with anger. 'This is no joking matter, Jacob.'

Jacob held up his hand. 'OK, I stand rebuked.'

Marie nodded and shrugged. 'So who will you take with you?'

'Young Pete and his pa. I believe Jeremiah Savage knows the place well.'

'But he's a lush, Jacob. How can you put trust in a lush in a saloon bar?'

'Well, like I told Pete, his father has been greatly underrated. He sure proved useful on our last trip. Without him we might all be lying on the slab in the funeral parlour right now.'

Marie shook her head. 'You're still as wild as ever despite your age, Jacob.'

'You make me sound like Methuselah!' he said with a smile. 'I'm still half way young. Would you have it any other way?'

'We're going to the Dee Vinery,' Jacob said to Jeremiah.

Jeremiah shrugged. 'It'll be an honour to accompany you, Mr Merriweather. But you know they're very free with the booze up there. You stand at the bar and they take down a bottle and push it to the end of the bar, and the barman at the other end uncorks it, and you can drink as much as you can take. I've seen guys fall down at the bar drunk as any English lord. Then they carry them outside and just lay them out like so many dead corpses. I've seen as many as six drunks lying there, just like they're set to stay there until kingdom come. It's a somewhat depressing sight, you know.'

Jacob grinned. 'Well, Mr Jeremiah Savage, I don't want to see you lying there for an instant. That doesn't fit into my plan. If that happens to you we'll leave you out there until you come round and shake it off.'

Jeremiah gave a deep chuckle. 'I shan't let a drop pass my lips, Mr Merriweather, not a drop, and that's a promise.'

Jacob and Pete and his father Jeremiah rode up through the hills until they reached the vinery. Jacob was amazed. The vines seemed to stretch out for ever across the gently undulating plains. The only human beings to be seen were men and occasionally women of colour tending the vines.

'So, now you see,' Jeremiah said, almost with a ring of mockery.

Pete, too, was amazed. 'Well, Boss, the owners of these vines must be as rich as that Greek guy Croesus.'

'This is where the money trees grow,' Jeremiah agreed. He pointed to a trail between the vines. 'The saloon is right at the end of the trail. Looks kind of inviting, don't it?'

The saloon at the end of the trail was a rather imposing building, like a Spanish hacienda. They rode up to it and dismounted. There were some half a dozen horses attached to the hitching rail, but no drunks lying on the ground or sitting on the benches outside. Inside there was a long bar with four bartenders in leather aprons in attendance doing their business. There was a pleasant aroma of combined cigar smoke and liquor, and a hum of voices, which reminded Jacob of a beehive about to swarm. When the three of them entered the saloon nobody took much notice of them, except for the odd nod and smile from the bartenders. One of the bartenders pushed a bottle towards them along the counter. Another uncorked the bottle with great dexterity and poured the wine into three glasses.

'Hi there, gents!' he said cheerfully. 'You come far?'

'Not so far,' Jacob said. He picked up his glass and sniffed the wine. 'What vintage?' he asked.

The bartender mentioned the year.

'That's quite a good vintage,' Jeremiah said.

The bartender scrutinized him closely. 'I believe I know you, sir. You've been here before. I never forget a face.'

'That was way back,' Jeremiah said. 'I've largely given up the bottle. Sort of reformed, you know.'

The barman chuckled. 'We don't have time to drink when we're on duty. It's too busy in here. You get sort of sick of it, anyway. The stink of booze gets right down inside you, and you can get pissed as a polecat without drinking a drop.'

Jacob opened his cigar case and offered it to the man. 'You got time to enjoy a good Havana cigar?'

The man shook his head. 'No, sir. I'm too busy right now.'

'Take one for later.'

'Well, thank you, sir. I do believe I will.' He took the offered cigar and put it behind his ear for later.

At that moment three dudes came into the bar and leaned against the counter, and the performance with the bottles continued.

'They must get through an awful lot of booze,' Pete said to his father.

Jeremiah shook his grey head. 'Good for business, my son. You can only hold so much liquor in your belly. These guys come in, and if they like it they place a big order.'

The bartender with the cigar behind his ear had a temporary reprieve, but still he didn't light up his cigar. He knew a first-class cigar when he met one.

'So, what do you want, sir?' he asked Jacob.

Jacob leaned across the counter. 'I want to talk to Mr Dickinson,' he said.

The man pulled a sceptical face. 'Why d'you want to talk to Mr Dickinson, sir?'

Jacob leaned even closer. 'A matter of business, sir.'

The bartender grinned. 'Well, sir, you won't find him here unless you hang around for six months or so, and I guess you won't want to do that, will you?'

Jacob placed a bundle of greenbacks on the counter close to the man's nose. 'Not if you can tell me where to find him.'

The bartender looked at the greenbacks as though he was tempted to take them, but wasn't quite sure whether it might compromise him. 'You must want to see Mr Dickinson awful bad, sir. And I see you and your buddies are packing hardware, too.' His eyes flicked over Pete and his father.

'Self defence,' Jacob told him. 'You can't be too careful these days, even in sunny California.'

'Well, sir, that may be true, but I wouldn't like to be the cause of any trouble around here. The days of shooting are largely over, you know.'

Jacob nodded. 'That might be so, sir, and if they are I'd be the happiest man in the world. But until I'm sure, I'll keep my gunbelt on.'

The barman looked down at the dollar bills. 'Well, you could try the big house, sir, but don't tell anyone I told you.'

Jacob stretched out his hand and grabbed back half the dollar bills. 'Thanks for your help, sir. I guess everyone knows about the big house, but thanks for being half helpful, anyway.' He pushed the dollars on the counter towards the bartender and stowed the rest in his vest pocket.

'Why did you do that?' Pete asked him when they were outside.

'Keep the opposition sweet,' Jacob said. 'A cigar and a handful of dollars can be just like a bowlful of sugar in that respect.'

Jeremiah chuckled.

They mounted up and turned away from the saloon. 'Where are we headed now?' Pete asked Jacob.

'Where else? We're going to the big house. It can't be far,' Jacob told him. They rode on between the vineyards, and the black workers doffed their hats with apparent respect. Jacob stopped once and asked the way to the big house and a burly black man straightened up and pointed a way in the distance. 'Mighty big house up there, sar. That's where the masters live when they're at home.'

'What do we aim to do?' Jeremiah asked Jacob.

'I'm going to ride right up to the front porch and dismount. You boys can stay where you are and wait until I come out again.'

'Is that wise, Boss?' Pete asked him.

'Wise or not, it's what we're going to do. So maybe it's good if you didn't take too much of that booze. This is no place for a booze-blind guy.'

Jacob swung down from his horse and stepped on to the wide porch where a black man was sitting on a rocking chair surveying the scene. 'Good day to you, sar,' the man said politely. 'Can I help you, sar?'

'You can tell me if Mr Dickinson is in.'

The man rose from the rocking chair and Jacob saw

that he was a giant. 'I'm not sure about that, sar. I'll just go into the house and check.' He looked down at Jacob. 'Maybe you should send in a card, sar.'

Jacob smiled politely. 'Just tell him it's Mr Merriweather, will you?'

'I sure will, sar. If I may say so, Merriweather's a mighty rich name.' He gave a low chuckle and then turned and disappeared inside the mansion.

Jacob turned and shouted over to Pete and Jeremiah. 'Take note of that, boys. This is a land of giants!'

After less than a minute the door of the mansion swung open again and the giant stood there looking down at Jacob.

'Master Dickinson asks you to name your business, sar. He's awful busy right now.'

'Did you tell him it was Jacob Merriweather to see him?'

The black man shook his head. 'I told him that. It don't make no difference, sar.'

'Maybe you should ask him again. Tell him I've come in answer to the notes he sent me.'

'The notes he sent you, sar?' The black man furrowed his brow in puzzlement.

'Yes. He wrote me several times.' Jacob mimed the business of writing and the black man gave him a broad and rather engaging smile. 'Yes, sar,' he said. 'I'll tell Mr Dickinson what you said.' He disappeared but returned again almost immediately. 'Sure you can come inside, Mr Merriweather, but we don't allow firearms in the house. So maybe you could just put your belt and guns on my bench so you can pick them up later.'

Jacob unbuckled his gunbelt and laid it on the bench. Then he turned to Pete and Jeremiah. 'See you later, boys.'

The big black man escorted Jacob into the house so closely that Jacob felt the man could have picked him up and put him in his pocket to snack on later. In the vast hallway, the man turned to him and said: 'Sit down, Mr Merriweather. Mr Dickinson, he be with you as soon as maybe.'

Jacob sat down on a chair that was more like a throne, and the black man sat opposite him on an equally imposing chair. Somewhere far away a clock chimed in sombre tones that sounded deeply menacing. The black man looked at Jacob with a long smile and a nod, but said nothing.

Jacob heard a door opening somewhere quite close and a man came walking towards him, and it was Fergus Walsh, all five foot six of him. As before, he was wearing a fancy vest, which emphasized his protuberant belly, as well as a number of elaborate rings on his fingers. The index finger of his right hand was missing.

Walsh came to a standstill some six feet away from Jacob. The huge black man stood up and looked down at them both as though they were no more than pawns on a chess board.

Walsh nodded and gave his not very pretty grin. 'Good day to you, Mr Merriweather. You've come an awful long way to see me. To what do I owe this pleasure?'

Jacob nodded and grinned. 'I've come to sort out a few misunderstandings between us, sir.'

Walsh looked momentarily puzzled. 'What misunderstandings would they be, Mr Merriweather?'

'The messages you sent me in the past few weeks.'

Walsh looked positively delighted. 'Well, Mr Merriweather, you surprise me, you really do.'

139

Jacob reached into his pocket for the notes, but Walsh turned to the huge black man and gave a nod of the head. The black man reached out and seized Jacob by the arm in a vicelike grip.

'Steady there, Josh!' Walsh said. 'We don't need to break the man's arm, do we? Listen before you act, that's what I always say.'

The huge black man chuckled indulgently and released Jacob's arm.

'Josh is only doing his duty, Mr Merriweather, but a man can't be too careful, can he, especially in the worst of all possible worlds?'

Jacob nodded and muttered, 'Voltaire, if I'm not mistaken.'

Walsh nodded. 'My, we are quick, aren't we, Mr Merriweather?'

'Except it's the best of all possible worlds,' Jacob retorted, 'as you well know, Mr Dickinson.'

Walsh gave a muted chuckle. 'We're dealing with an educated man here, Josh, you know that?'

The black man grinned and nodded: he hadn't a clue what his master was talking about.

'Let the man reach into pocket, Josh,' Walsh instructed.

'Yes, sar.'

Jacob reached into his pocket and produced the notes Dickinson had sent him. Walsh, alias Dickinson, took them in his hand and glanced through them. 'Well, well, well,' he said. 'The Alamo, Custer's last stand, and what happened at the Ford Theatre the night Lincoln was assassinated. These notes have one thing in common, don't they?'

'You should know, you sent them,' Jacob replied.

'Ha, ha!' Walsh laughed. 'You should have been a Thespian, Mr Merriweather.'

'Instead of which I wound up as a lawyer.'

Walsh held up a finger. 'Much the same thing, sir, much the same thing. But enough of these pleasantries. We have work to do, don't we?'

'What work would that be, Mr Walsh?'

Walsh spread his hands and shrugged. 'Why, your trial, Mr Merriweather, your trial, of course.'

Jacob shook his head. 'I don't think you can be serious, Mr Walsh. If anyone's going on trial it's you, not me.'

Walsh gave his somewhat unpleasant grin. 'You're a very clever lawyer, Mr Merriweather, and you have a fine taste in cigars, but you haven't yet learned to call a spade a spade, have you?' He turned to the big black man. 'Josh, be kind enough to look outside and see what's happening, will you?'

'Yes, sar.' The black man made towards the door, but he didn't get far. The door swung open and Pete and Jeremiah were thrust inside at gunpoint. Behind them stood two gunmen, one of them Chuck Clarkson. Pete looked decidedly shamefaced and Jeremiah was fuming with anger. 'They got the drop on us, Boss,' Pete said apologetically.

'I'm sorry I got you into this, boys,' Jacob said. He turned to Walsh. 'What happens now?'

'Well, sir, now we take a short ride to the courthouse. It isn't too far, I assure you. Not nearly as far as Babylon, and we don't need candlelight to get there, either.' He looked at the big black man and chuckled, and the black man chuckled back, though he still had no idea what his employer was talking about.

'Who's on trial, and what's the charge?' Pete asked boldly.

Walsh gave his whinnying laugh again. 'You've got a lot to learn, boy. Like when to keep that big mouth of yours shut.' He turned to the black man. 'Josh, will you give this boy a lesson in keeping his mouth shut.'

'I sure will, sar.' The black man took Pete by the shoulders and twisted him round like a teetotum; then he struck him across the mouth with such force that he fell to the ground.

'Thank you, Josh,' Dickinson purred.

Jeremiah made to leap forwards, but the black man struck him forcefully with his huge fist and Jeremiah fell back and struck his head on the floor.

'Oh dear,' Walsh exclaimed. 'That means blood on the carpet! Another job for you to do, Josh.'

'Sure thing, sar.' The black man grinned. He seemed free from malice and content to do his job. If Walsh had ordered him to garrot a man or cut his throat he'd have done it with a smile.

Jacob looked down at young Pete and his pa and made sure they were still breathing. In fact, Pete sat up and retched and spat out two of his teeth.

'More mess on the carpet,' Fergus Walsh complained.

'That was a brutal thing to do,' Jacob said.

Walsh cum Dickinson chuckled again. 'It's what comes of keeping bad company, Mr Merriweather.'

Jacob shook his head. 'These two boys never did anyone any harm.'

'Well, Mr Merriweather, it would be a good idea to save your lip for later. You're sure gonna need it for your defence.'

142

Jacob shook his head. 'I don't know what you think you're doing, but you won't get away with it, because all my friends know where we are.'

Walsh gave that sinister cackling laugh again. 'Your friends and relations might know where you were headed, but I don't think they'll follow you to hell and back in case they get themselves badly burned.'

'You'd be surprised,' Jacob said.

Walsh turned to the black man. 'Josh, give the man a gentle tap to show him we're not fooling around here.'

The black man reached out and gripped Jacob by the arm and twirled him round. Then he gave him a tap on the forehead with his massive fist. But it wasn't hard enough to do any real damage or knock him out cold. Jacob stared Josh in the eye and Josh gave him a reassuring grin.

Pete and his pa dragged themselves up from the floor. Both had blood on their lips.

'That's better,' Walsh cum Dickinson said. 'Now you're ready, we're gonna take a short ride. Take them to the door, boys. The carriage should be waiting. Only the best . . . only the best for our guests. After all, we're not brutes, are we? Oh, by the way, I forgot to mention my sister, didn't I? She'll be waiting for us in the courthouse.'

At the foot of the steps a long black carriage was drawn up. It was as if they were going to a funeral, Jacob thought.

'D'you think they aim to kill us?' Pete asked through his blood-swollen lips.

'Best to keep quiet,' Jacob told him. 'The more you say, the more danger you'll be in.'

'I'll kill those bastards if I get half a chance,' Jeremiah muttered.

'Try to be invisible,' Jacob advised him. 'The less you say, the better your chances are.'

The door of the carriage opened, and Josh, the black man, squeezed himself in. And it sure was a squeeze!

Jacob looked across at Josh and shook his head.

'How did you get yourself into this mess?' Jacob asked the black man.

Josh grinned. 'It just came naturally by being so big and strong. Mr Dickinson just picked me out and that suited me just fine. And I'm not supposed to talk to you. If I hurt you boys I'm real sorry, but that's just the way it is.'

Jacob looked at Jeremiah and Jeremiah took the hint. He was still only half conscious from the blow he'd received.

After less than half an hour they came to a barn. Josh got out of the carriage, which was a relief, since Jacob and the other two could breathe more easily.

'You get out here,' the black man said. He stood at the foot of the carriage and Jacob got out, followed by the other two. 'Now you go into the court room,' Josh said.

Jacob and Pete and Pete's father walked into the barn, which was surprisingly big inside. Everything was arranged just like a genuine court of law. There were seats facing a platform on which was a table, behind which was a throne-like seat.

'You set yourself down here,' Josh said to Jacob. 'The other two gents sit over there, out of the way.'

Jacob sat down at the front facing the thronelike chair and Josh plonked himself down beside him.

There was a long moment of suspense. Jacob felt an almost irresistible urge to laugh, but he knew he was in a difficult, if not desperate situation, and that laughter could make things a whole lot worse. So he sat still and awaited developments.

From somewhere a voice boomed out: 'Be upstanding for her honour the judge.'

'This is where you get yourself on your feet,' Josh said, jerking Jacob up by his elbow.

A diminutive figure appeared from the back of the barn. It mounted the steps, bowed towards the chairs to the right and left, and then sat down on the throne. It was, in fact, a woman, and Jacob recognized her at once as Mrs Walsh, the wife that Walsh cum Dickinson had supposedly wanted to get rid of. She waved everyone to be seated.

Jacob remained standing. 'What's the meaning of this farce?' he demanded.

'Silence in court!' someone shouted.

'Sit down, Mr Merriweather,' Mrs Walsh said.

Josh took Jacob by the arm and pulled him down on to his seat. By the black man's standards it was a gentle pull, but Jacob landed on the seat with an undignified plonk.

Mrs Walsh smiled and nodded. 'That's better. Now the Clerk of the Court will read the indictment.'

A man sitting below the so-called judge's chair got to his feet and cleared his throat somewhat pompously. Then, looking at nobody in particular, he read the so-called indictment in a high, hillbilly voice. Once again Jacob felt strongly tempted to laugh, but got to his feet and again said:

'Excuse me, but what is the meaning of this farce?'

Mrs Walsh held up her hand. 'The accused will be silent and listen to the indictment!'

Josh pulled Jacob down abruptly again and said in his

145

ear. 'Best to be quiet, man. Things are better that way.'

Jacob sat still and listened to the rambling, monotonous voice of the accuser.

According to the indictment Jacob had made the original accusation against the rancher Jack Dickinson, and when Dickinson had been found not guilty, he had broken into his ranch house and shot Dickinson and his manservant dead. At the end of this monotonous rambling the so-called lawyer sat down and wiped his brow with a spotted handkerchief.

Mrs Walsh stared directly at Jacob. 'How do you plead, prisoner at the bar?'

Jacob didn't attempt to get up again. He laughed and said, 'I don't plead at all.'

'You must plead guilty or not guilty,' she said.

'This is just a whole cartload of rubbish!' Jeremiah was on his feet and shouted through his broken teeth.

'Be quiet, sir!' the so-called judge shouted in reply.

Jeremiah snorted and sat down, and Pete muttered to him to keep quiet.

Mrs Walsh fixed a relentless gaze on Jacob. 'Do you deny killing Jack Dickinson and his butler?'

Jacob shook his head. 'I neither deny nor affirm it, but I should warn you – you are not above the law. A number of men have already been killed because of you, and quite soon the law of the land will catch up with you, and you will be punished. And then all the vineries in California won't be able to help, because you'll be doing a long stretch in jail.'

Mrs Walsh glanced to her left where her husband was sitting. Then she returned her gaze to Jacob. 'So you deny the charges, Jacob Merriweather?'

Jacob shook his head and grinned. 'I neither affirm them nor deny them.'

'In that case,' she said, 'I must sentence you to a contest of strength.'

'What does that mean?'

'It means you must wrestle with Josh here . . . and if you survive, the better for you. If not . . . well, that's just too bad, isn't it?'

Jacob glanced sideways at Josh and Josh nodded and smiled a not unfriendly smile. 'I guess that's the way it has to be, sar,' he said.

CHAPTER TEN

This farce had obviously been planned beforehand. In very short order the so-called courthouse had been transformed into a kind of wrestling ring, and Jacob knew he couldn't escape from this mediaeval contest. Though Josh smiled, it was the smile of a Goliath who knew he was invincible, particularly as Jacob wasn't David, and he had no sling and there were no pebbles handy, anyway. So all he had was his wits and his bare hands, and right now they both felt somewhat weak and befuddled.

'What are we going to do, Boss?' Pete asked him.

'Like always, I'm going to do my best,' Jacob said, trying not to betray his fear.

'Let me stand in for you,' Jeremiah offered bravely. 'I know a thing or two about hand-to-hand fighting.'

'Thanks for the offer, but I don't think so,' Jacob said. 'This is my bag, and I have to shape up to him or die. That's just the way it is.' He looked across at the big black man and saw that Josh was stretching his arms high above his head and then flexing his huge bicep muscles like Samson about to bring down the temple. 'Just remember this,' he said to Pete. 'Take in every detail so that when you get out of this mess you can tell the tale just as it happened.'

'I sure will, Boss,' Pete assured him. 'That is, if I do get out of it.'

'Don't you worry, Mr Merriweather,' Jeremiah assured Jacob. 'There's a way out of every forest, and we're gonna find it. No fears about that.'

Actually, Jacob had considerable fears about that, especially when he looked over at the huge black man and saw him beckoning to him.

'Keep cool and think,' he said to himself. Then despite his growing apprehension he noted that Josh had a loose waistcoat and a wide belt, both of which could be useful in hand-to-hand fighting. Though the man's arms were long, they weren't so long that he could keep Jacob at bay. Another thing Jacob noted was that like most big people, Josh wasn't exactly nimble on his feet.

Before Jacob could make a further assessment, the giant came storming towards him with a deep growling noise like an angry grizzly bear.

At that point most men would have frozen with terror which would mean being picked up like a straw doll and hurled to the other end of the room, and that would have been the end of the conflict. But although Jacob was old he was still reasonably nimble and fast. So as the giant lumbered in, he skipped to one side to avoid coming into contact with those huge meaty fists, and as Josh drew level with him, he grabbed his loose jacket and stuck out his leg to trip him up. Josh plunged forward on to one knee, reaching out to save himself. Then he blundered right into a chair, which disintegrated under his weight.

Jacob knew if he wasted a moment the giant would be

on his feet again, fuming with rage. There were no Queensberry rules in this contest: a man either lost or won, and if he lost it was curtains for him. So he lunged forwards and booted the giant as hard as he could in the rear end. At the same moment Jeremiah grabbed a leg of the broken chair and struck Josh across the back of the head as hard as he could.

That would have finished a normal man, but Josh was no normal man. He thrust Jeremiah aside like a leaf with a sweep of his hand, then staggered to his feet and turned to face Jacob with a roar of fury.

Jacob was panting for breath, but a voice deep inside him said, 'Don't falter, man. Keep going if you want to live.' So he didn't think, he acted instinctively. As the giant bore down on him, he risked getting inside those fists and struck out with the blade of his hand across Josh's throat. Josh stopped with a choking gasp, and Jacob followed this up by kneeing him in the crutch. The giant doubled up with a choking gasp and Jacob struck him on the back of his neck. Josh fell forwards and lay shuddering and choking. To make sure, Jeremiah sprang to his feet and struck Josh again twice with the chair leg.

'Take that, you bastard!' he shouted. There was a pulpy thud as Josh fell forwards.

Jacob knew he had no time to relax. So he swung round gasping, and staggered towards Dickinson's heavies. Chuck Clarkson was staring at Jacob in astonishment, and Dickinson was looking even more amazed. Jacob tried to run forwards, but the fight had knocked the breath out of him. The only one who had enough energy to move forwards quickly was young Pete Savage, and he ran like a wolf straight at Chuck Clarkson. Clarkson was trying to draw his weapon as Pete butted him full in the face, and Clarkson fell back against a chair with blood streaming from a broken nose. Pete didn't waste a second. He reached down and grabbed Clarkson's gun and jerked it free. Then he sprang away and cocked it and held it forward to cover Dickinson. As he did so, his father Jeremiah rushed in and struck another of the heavies with the chair leg.

Pete levelled the gun at Davidson and shouted, 'Anyone move, and this guy gets a bullet through his head.'

There was a moment of confused silence.

'Do as he says,' Davidson ordered.

'All of you raise your hands above your heads where I can see them' – Pete waved the gun towards them – 'and that includes the so-called lady judge.'

A small forest of hands shot up.

'Good work, my son,' Jeremiah said, as he went about relieving them of their guns, including the judge, who turned out to be Walsh-cum-Dickinson's sister, not his wife.

Jeremiah handed Jacob a gun with a gleam of satisfaction in his eye. Jacob turned towards Josh, just as Josh struggled to get to his feet. The black man, who had turned a strange shade of green, tried to speak, but all that came out was a croak. He was in such bad shape that he couldn't help but fall back on a chair again.

Jacob walked forwards and prodded him with the gun. 'Well, at least you're still alive, Josh, and I'm glad I didn't have to kill you.'

Josh tried to smile, but it ended in a grimace. Then he stretched out his hand as if to shake with Jacob.

'No, thank you,' Jacob said. 'Enough is enough for one day. Just thank God you're still in the land of the living.'

Josh held up one arm in compliance. His right hand was busy trying to relieve the bruising on his throat.

'What happens now?' the so-called judge asked in a tremulous tone close to tears.

'What happens now is you go back to town and face the real law of the land, and that is Merriweather's law as well. And for your information, I did not kill Jack Dickinson and his butler all those years ago, though I did prosecute Dickinson for killing two innocent young people who were just trying to earn an honest living on their farm.' Then he turned to Fergus Walsh-cum-Dickinson.

'As for you, sir, you must be the biggest fool in the whole of California and western America. When you came to my office and tried to implicate me in the murder of your wife you said you owned a silver mine. Now I see you own a huge vinery that must be worth millions. But because the devil has burrowed right into your rotten soul you've put that huge fortune at risk and sacrificed the lives of at least three men. And now you've reached the end of the trail, sir. You'd better put your wealth towards employing the best lawyer in California for your defence, because you're sure going to need him.'

Having relieved Dickinson and his sister and all the heavies of their weapons, Jeremiah went about tying their hands behind their backs, whistling to himself with satisfaction as he did so. Among his other skills, Jeremiah had a way with knots, and he obviously enjoyed employing it.

Jacob covered Josh with his newly acquired gun. The giant was still somewhat green in the face and couldn't

talk, but pointed to his throat and gave a series of inartic-
ulate grunts.

'Don't worry, Uncle,' Jeremiah said somewhat unsym-
pathetically. 'You're lucky to be alive, man.'

Josh grunted and nodded in agreement and submitted
placidly to having his hands tied.

The whole cavalcade then mounted up and started
their journey towards town.

'What do we do for food?' Dickinson asked glumly.

'You'll be fed soon enough,' Jacob said. 'And you can
pay for the best caviar in town, if that's to your taste. In the
meantime, you drink when we stop to feed and water the
horses.'

They rode on down the trail that led from the
Dickinson mansion between the vines towards the saloon,
and then on towards town. As they rode on they passed
many black men and women working on the vines. The
workers looked up in amazement and shaded their eyes
against the sun. Dickinson and his sister stared steadfastly
ahead.

'Is this some kind of play acting?' one of the women
asked with a huge smile.

Josh would have liked to reply, but all he could do was
shake his head.

'Well, it sure ain't Blind Man's Bluff!' Jeremiah said.

When they reached town, all the store owners came out to
gawp in wonder. The workers working on Cy Clavell's
emporium downed tools and stared in amazement, and Cy
Clavell himself appeared on the sidewalk. 'Well, I'll be
damned!' he said. And all the guests of The Silversmith
Hotel were there lining the sidewalk, including Marie and

the manager Trent Oldsmere.

Marie raised her skirts and ran along the sidewalk to keep pace with the procession, and Jacob drew rein and dismounted. Although neither of them cared for public displays of emotion, this was an exception, and they embraced right there on the sidewalk, and everybody cheered. Further down the street Oscar Savage and Dorothy stood hand in hand grinning with delight.

The town jail was somewhat small and cramped, so the prisoners from the Dickinson mansion had to crowd into two small cells, except for Dickinson's sister, who had a cell to herself. After all, she was a woman, if not a lady.

'I demand better treatment!' Dickinson complained. 'You can't treat innocent folk like this!'

'Well,' Jacob said. 'I'm afraid you can't have the royal suite. It's already taken.'

Several people laughed, but Dickinson shook his head and frowned. 'You know this was all a joke,' he insisted. 'We never meant to harm you.'

'Keep that for the judge,' Jacob said. 'Maybe he has a taste for fairy tales.'

Jacob then went to Doc Deacon's infirmary to give his friend Ed Mullins the lowdown on events. Ed was still none too fit, but he was making good progress; he might have been small-boned and short, but he had true grit. 'What do we do now?' he asked Jacob.

'You send a wire through to the judge, and give him all the facts. Give him something useful to chew on before he retires.'

CHAPTER ELEVEN

After the legitimate trial of Fergus Walsh-cum-Dickinson, Marie was so pleased with the outcome she decided to throw a big party involving everyone who had taken part in the famous 'Battle of the Vines', as it came to be known later, including Cy Clavell and his timid wife, and Jeremiah Savage and his wife who was by no means timid, and his sons Pete and Oscar, and Oscar's betrothed Dorothy. Jacob Junior and his two sisters were also present. Fortunately, Ed Mullins was well enough to attend with his wife.

Marie hired a small band, and they played a sort of honky tonk music which everyone seemed to enjoy. There was dancing and singing, and everyone became slightly intoxicated and somewhat riotous. The event was enjoyed by everyone, except those behind bars, of course!

When the band paused to tip back well earned drinks, Cy Clavell called for order. 'Mr Merriweather and I have a few announcements to make,' he said. 'Isn't that so, Jacob?'

'Indeed it is,' Jacob agreed. He stood up and looked around at the guests. 'Dear friends,' he said, 'this has been a tough time for us all.' He turned to the Savage family. 'Without Jeremiah and his two sons I'd most probably be speaking at my own funeral by now, so to speak.'

'Here, here!' someone shouted, and everyone laughed. But then Cy Clavell stood up and started clapping heartily and everyone joined in.

Jacob held up his hand again. 'Mr Clavell and I have been conferring together, and we've come to a decision.'

'That's right,' Cy Clavell agreed.

'With the help of our wives, of course,' Jacob said.

More laughter. Jacob Junior and his sisters started clapping vigorously. 'Sure thing!' young Jacob shouted unabashed.

'What's the decision?' Trent Oldsmere shouted.

'OK,' Jacob said. 'We've decided that this town needs a theatre, a place of entertainment. . . .' He paused for dramatic effect, and everyone listened intently . . . 'It will be called . . . The Oscar and Peter Playhouse, and the manager will be . . . Jeremiah Savage!'

There was a stunned silence, and then Pete and Oscar cheered so loudly that they almost brought the house down.

'Thank you, Boss!' they shouted in unison.

'Except you won't be running the show, Oscar, because you'll be too busy studying law at law school.'

'Why, thank you, Boss.' Oscar looked suitably abashed, and Dorothy squeezed his hand under the table.

'And of course, Mr Peter Savage will be in charge of productions.'

Another cheer, in which Peter Savage somewhat immodestly joined.

*

'So,' Cy Clavell said to Jacob later, 'What about Gunfighters of the Old West? Are you ready to be included now? After all, everyone knows about 'The Battle of the Vines'. You and the boys are famous throughout the whole state of California and beyond.'

Jacob smiled. 'Let's just wait and see what happens, shall we?'

'You could wait for ever and a day, my friend. Time waits for no man,' Cy Clavell said. 'And there could be money in it, as I said earlier.'

'Well,' Jacob said, 'someone once said the love of money is the root of all evil, and I'd sooner be remembered as a good lawyer than a gunman. Those men I killed will always rise up to haunt me in my dreams.'

'Self defence, sir, self defence. And anyway, what's happened has happened, and you can't make it unhappen. So you might as well make the best of it, my friend.'

Jacob nodded. 'You have the very devil's way of tempting a man, Cy. So I'll make a bargain with you. If we can put Dickinson behind bars for a long spell, I'll think about letting you publish my story.'

'Well, that's very generous, my friend, but since all this will be in the news-sheets, anyway, you may as well benefit from it. Don't you agree?'

Jacob nodded. 'Maybe so,' he said.

Dickinson didn"t suffer much in the town jail. Though the mattress was a bit lumpy he ordered the best food possible to be brought in from the hotel, and while he didn't get caviar, his waistline didn't exactly reduce, either. In fact without exercise he grew more corpulent than ever. Of course, he had enough money tucked away to hire the best lawyers available, but Jacob had accumulated a lot of experience and friends over the years, and he was also able to employ excellent lawyers.

After a long battle in the courts Dickinson went down for five years, which was quite a light sentence considering his crimes. His sister was set free unconditionally. Dickinson's heavies went down for somewhat longer.

Dickinson's lawyers suggested that Jacob had deliberately provoked Dickinson, but Jacob's lawyers had the notes that Dickinson had sent to Jacob read out in court, and apart from causing a good deal of laughter, they clinched the matter.

In fact five years in jail wasn't too much of a hardship for Dickinson, since he still retained his assets. So he was able to live in style and grow even fatter!

Then there was Josh, the giant black man. He recovered from the chop to the throat which might have killed a weaker man, though his voice became more of a growl than ever. As he had committed no crime, he was released. And he was not a revengeful man: he had a forgiving and sunny nature.

Some time after the trial Dorothy looked into Jacob's office. 'Excuse me, Boss, but there's a man to see you.'

'Did he state his business?'

'No, Boss, he just growled at me and said he wanted to see Mr Merriweather. I must warn you he's very big and very black. Shall I send him away?'

'No, Dorothy. Please send him in.'

Josh appeared at the door immediately, and gave Jacob a huge smile, and then scowled. 'I'm Josh,' he said. 'You probably remember me?'

Jacob looked at him and chuckled. 'How could I forget you, Josh, especially since you very nearly killed me.'

'You be a hard man to kill, Mr Merriweather.'

'Well, we both survived, so I guess we both have something to be thankful for.'

'Yes, sur,' Josh said.

There was a pause.

'So why don't you sit down and tell me what I can do for, Josh?'

Josh looked round the room uncertainly. Then he parked himself on a chair. 'Well, it's like this, Mr Merriweather: since the master is in prison, I lost my job, and I ain't got nothin to do and nowhere to go, you see.'

Jacob nodded slowly. 'I do see . . . I do see. Have you got a family?'

Josh smiled again. 'I sure do, sur, a lady wife and two children, a boy and a girl.'

Jacob considered a moment. 'How are you around horses, Josh?'

'Well, I do like the horses, Mr Merriweather, and they seem to be OK around me.'

Jacob nodded. 'Well, that's good, because we need someone to care for the horses at The Silversmith Hotel. So sit down and I'll have someone bring lunch, and then we'll walk right up to the hotel and talk to my wife about it.'

'That's real kind of you, Mr Merriweather, real kind.'

Not everything ends happily for everyone, but at least it ended happily for Josh, and Jacob was content too.